PANCAKES, BACON & A SIDE OF MURDER

A TEXAS-SIZED MURDER MYSTERY

BY KERI LYNN

Scrivenings
PRESS
Quench your thirst for story.
www.ScriveningsPress.com

Published by Scrivenings Press LLC
15 Lucky Lane
Morrilton, Arkansas 72110
https://ScriveningsPress.com

Printed in the United States of America

Paperback ISBN 978-1-64917-139-9

eBook ISBN 978-1-64917-140-5

Library of Congress Control Number: 2021942375

Cover by Linda Fulkerson
www.bookmarketinggraphics.com

Scripture are taken from the KING JAMES VERSION (KJV): KING JAMES VERSION, public domain.

All characters are fictional, and any resemblance to real people, either factual or historical, is purely coincidental.

To all who dream.

ACKNOWLEDGMENTS

Thank you to everyone at Scrivenings Press who helped make this dream turn into reality. This has been an incredible adventure to embark on.

1

Finding the dead body of Victoria Phillips wasn't exactly how I had planned on starting my day. Especially only ten minutes after eating my second strawberry-mango donut.

Victoria—or Vicki—ran the diner across the street from mine. We'd been rivals from the day we'd opened our stores in Flamingo Springs, Texas, which, subsequently, happened to be on the same day. Both offering the deal of All You Can Eat Pancakes for $3. In all fairness though, Vicki had copied my ideas, not the other way around. Originally, she was scheduled to open a week after me, but moved it up to the same day to try to outdo me, which was also why she'd put the same coupon in the paper.

Staring down at where she lay on her stomach on the sparkling blue floor of her kitchen, I swayed. Shaking, I dug my cell phone from my pocket and dialed 9-1-1, knowing from the grotesque way her neck was twisted there was nothing I could do for her. I congratulated myself on being calm, until I noticed the dark pool of blood slowly drying around her blond head.

"9-1-1, what's your emergency?" Terri Townshend's powerful voice filled my ear.

It took a few tries before I managed to squeak out, "Terri, it's —it's, Aubrey."

"Aubrey?" Terri's voice sharpened, and I could imagine her sitting straight up in her chair, one hand flying to her generous bosom. "Are you all right? Tell me what's wrong."

"I—I'm in Vicki's kitchen, and—and," my words broke off as I started to sob. "Oh, my word, Terri, she's dead! Someone killed her."

Terri said something, but I couldn't understand what through the rushing noise that pounded in my ears. It wasn't until she'd shouted my name repeatedly that I heard her.

"I'm sending the sheriff," she said. "You sit tight, don't touch anything, and stay on the line. If you feel at all unsafe, get out of there. Do you understand me?"

"Yes," I whispered, still staring at the lifeless form of my archenemy. Blood pooled by her shoulder, staining her neatly coiffed hair. I could only imagine what she would say when she woke up, as Vicki really prided herself on her hair. I leaned against the wall, hearing Terri breathe into my ear as I realized I was going into shock. My stomach threatened to give me back my breakfast, and I swallowed hard, hoping I didn't vomit.

Well, until I saw what was sticking out from under Vicki's chest—something she'd obviously clutched against her when the killing blow had been delivered: my secret recipe book. In fact, it was the very one I kept locked in a vault in my own bakery, a book filled with recipes and measurements that took me years to collect and create. Vicki found out about the book only days after I opened, overhearing me talking about it to a friend when she dropped by to see what type of special I was serving, and she'd never stopped trying to get her hands on it. First, she tried to bribe me, then threaten me, and lastly, she tried to pay my waitress to steal it. For the briefest of moments,

I wished she were still alive for the simple reason that I could slug her right in her perfectly made-up face. I didn't think the police would find it acceptable for me to do it now, since she was dead.

Hearing a noise at the front of the pink and green dining area, I let out a squeak, Terri's warning suddenly sinking in that I could be in danger as well.

"That's just Blaze," she assured me. "Now honey, I'm getting off the line, but once this is over, I'll be waiting for you at your diner, okay?"

The room spun around me, and I dropped my phone to the floor where it landed with a clatter. When it settled into the pool of blood, my equilibrium decided it was a good time to take a vacation. I swayed forward as Blaze, the new sheriff of Flamingo Springs, came through the swinging door, one hand on his gun. Boot heels sounding loud in the somber silence, he strode forward, the scent of his cologne filling my nose.

He grabbed my arm and pulled me across the room. We were almost through the door before my stomach came up with the brilliant idea to reject my breakfast. Letting out a belch, I leaned forward and deposited the contents of my guts right on his boots. The last thing I saw was my own puke coming up to greet my face as I tipped forward.

And then, there was nothing.

"I'm going to need you to tell me again exactly what you saw and did when you came into Vicki's Creations, and why you were here."

Blaze pinned me with a hard stare, green eyes dark as they met my pale blue ones.

"And while you're at it, you can tell me why she has a recipe book with your name on it in her arms."

Biting back a groan, I pulled the blanket he'd given me closer around my shoulders, even though it had to be pushing ninety degrees outside. I was seated on a metal Victorian chair painted an obscene shade of bright pink. When I focused on the table in front of me, the surface cleared of its vase of fresh flowers and dainty menus for Blaze's hat and laptop, I found the lime green to be just as hard on my eyes.

"I already told you three times what happened," I snapped at Blaze, shifting in my chair, jean-clad legs rubbing together. It'd been less than an hour since I found Vicki, and already, I felt like the case was closed. Like it was only a matter of time before I was forced to take a mug shot, which was ridiculous. We might be enemies, but there was no way I would have ever killed Vicki, even though there were times I could have planted my boot in her rear.

Blaze stabbed at a key on his laptop and looked back up. "Humor me, and tell me one more time." His voice was gruff.

I think he was still a bit peeved over me upchucking on his boots, even though he managed to keep me from faceplanting on them. I don't know why that would upset him, though, since they washed off quite nicely outside with a water hose.

I took a deep breath, pinching the bridge of my nose between my fingers. "I told you, she always opens exactly thirteen minutes before me every day, like she has been for the last two years, because that makes perfect sense in her world. She says the breakfast crowd will come to her and not me that way, but I've never noticed that to be true." I paused to collect my thoughts. "When I went to turn on the open sign this morning, I looked across the street and saw she was still closed. That's totally not like—" I swallowed hard, doing my best to not look over Blaze's shoulder toward the kitchen, where I knew Vicki was still laying as Jeff, Flamingo Springs' doctor, made his examination, occasionally muttering under his breath. "That wasn't like her," I went on, finally shifting my gaze to the glossy black floor.

"And then what did you do?" Blaze asked, pecking at his keyboard, the scent of his limey cologne wafting across the table at me as the AC kicked on.

Staring at the table, I replied, "I thought something might be wrong, like maybe she'd fallen or something. Just last week, I slipped on some spilled butter and almost cracked my head op—" I felt the blood leave my face, and for the first time, Blaze showed a hint of compassion.

"And you thought the same thing might have happened to her, since she never hired anyone to help out, so there would be no one to check on her," he finished for me, typing out a few more words.

Nodding, I looked up. "Yeah. I mean, even though we didn't like each other, we still looked out for one another. The one day I opened late last year, she came over and pounded on the door to make sure I wasn't sick. She told me no one was trustworthy enough to work for her, and that's why she never hired anyone, so I tried to keep an eye out for her."

"And when you went into the kitchen, you found her on the floor, with your recipe book clutched in her arms." Blaze leaned back in his chair, focusing on me, and I found myself unable to meet his harsh stare. I settled for staring at his throat, made visible because he'd left the top two buttons of his tan shirt undone. The patch with the police emblem was fixed right above his heart, a pen stuck in the pocket just below it.

"Yeah," I said. "That's my secret recipe compilation." I shuddered as I remembered the blood splattered across the spine of my treasured book and wondered if it would come out of paper.

"Which you've said on multiple occasions that you keep hidden, locked up, because it holds the recipes of your famous pancakes and those weird jalapeño chocolate things."

"Dragon's Breath cupcakes," I corrected him, and his brow

lowered. "But I have no idea why Vicki had it, or how she even got it. I keep it in a vault in the bakery kitchen!"

Blaze stared at me for a long moment, and I resisted the urge to wipe my sweaty palms on my blue T-shirt, knowing that would make me look guilty, though of what, I didn't know. He couldn't possibly be thinking *I'd* murdered Vicki. Could he?

"So, to reiterate, you found Vicki dead in her own kitchen with your secret recipe book still in her arms, something you two have fought over since you both opened two years ago, killed by a single blow to the head, the weapon most likely a rolling pin—something you look like you're strong enough to do—and you're telling me you have no idea how the victim got like this?"

Flabbergasted at what he was suggesting, it took a moment for it to sink in, but when it did, I stood. Dropping the blanket from my shoulders, I ignored Stetson, the town's only deputy, as he moved past us with a camera, having finally taken enough crime scene shots. Glaring down at the sheriff with all the fire and vinegar I possessed, which, after being accused of murder, wasn't much, I took a breath.

"How dare you even suggest that I would do such a horrible thing—"

"Sit down, Ms. Turner." Blaze never even batted an eye at my display, only stared at me with cool eyes. It was as if he'd already condemned me of the crime and locked me in prison, throwing the key in the garbage on his way out.

Though I swayed a bit, I stood my ground. My mouth filled with the bitter taste that comes from having regurgitated coffee. "I will not! Now, you—"

"You either sit, or I will seat you." Blaze never moved, but one look at the shoulders wide as a barn and the fact he outweighed me by a good fifty pounds had me quietly retaking my seat. He leaned forward. "Now, Ms. Turner,"

"Aubrey," I interrupted him snappishly. "Ms. Turner is reserved for those who treat me with respect!"

"Aubrey," he ground out, "I never accused you of anything, I simply stated the obvious, which, if you forget, is my job. Now, I'm going to ask you some more questions, and you will answer them without moving from your chair. Are we clear?"

Pulling the blanket back around me, I gave him a small nod. He shut the laptop and pushed it to the side of the table, arms folded in front of him, biceps straining at his long sleeves. Unlike Flamingo Springs' last sheriff, Mason Rogers, who liked his beer and loved his cupcakes, Blaze Martin kept himself in good shape. Not that I was noticing or anything. I totally wasn't.

"Where were you between the time of 12:30 a.m. and 1:45 a.m. this morning?"

"At home, of course. Why?"

Blaze drummed the fingers of his right hand on his left forearm. "Just answer the question. I'm interviewing you, not the other way around."

"I did," I snapped. "Or are you that hard of hearing?"

To his credit, Blaze ignored my question and went on. "And what were you doing at that time?"

"Yoga," I responded, my mind momentarily wondering if Brey, my more than part-time but not quite full-time help had opened my shop yet. The brunch crowd would be moving through soon, if they hadn't already.

"Yoga," Blaze repeated, leaning back in his chair, arms over his chest. I fought to not stare as his shoulders flexed. "At one in the morning?"

I could hear the disbelief in his voice, and though I really wanted to climb on top of the table and give him a piece of my mind for looking at me like I was crazy, I remembered his warning and answered. "Yes, yoga. I work out when I have the time, and that was when I had time yesterday." I frowned. "Or today. Whichever."

He stretched his legs out under the table, boots nudging my sneakers. "You were doing yoga, at one in the morning, which is around the time Jeff says Vicki was killed. Was anyone with you?"

Blowing out a breath, I ran a hand through my hair. I'd started my day with it in a neat French twist, and already, it had managed to mostly come free, probably from when I'd passed out in the arms of the rather grumpy sheriff.

"Aubrey, if someone was with you, I need to know. Nothing you tell me will leave this interview."

Letting out a heavy sigh, I contemplated not admitting someone was with me that night. Not because, like Blaze was probably assuming, I had a secret lover, which, I mean, I wouldn't argue if I did. I don't know the last time I had a date. But it wasn't that. It was something far more embarrassing.

Pulling my feet under my chair so that they no longer touched Blaze's boots, I leaned forward. Boots, I might add, that were attached to mile long legs I'd admired from afar more than once. But that's beside the point. "There was someone with me," I admitted.

Before Blaze could open his mouth a voice said, "And that someone was me."

I didn't even have to turn to know that Misty Von Oepen, my best friend and owner of Soul Yoga, had entered the building. She sat next to me in a vacant chair that was just as pink as the rest of the dining area, a cloud of lavender rising from her as she did so. "I was with her, Blaze, helping her with a pose."

Blaze's eyes darted between us, taking in Misty's broomstick skirt, pink hair, and feather earrings. After a pause, he said, "Okay, so, you were with Aubrey this morning, helping her with a ... yoga pose, from midnight to almost two?" Disbelief was evident in his voice, clearly thinking we were lying.

But with a gentle smile, Misty replied, "Yes. Aubrey recently started following a rather strenuous exercise program, and when she complained about being stiff, I suggested she take up practicing yoga at night to relieve the tension. She called me after she got turned around doing a pose."

At Blaze's blank look, I hurried to add, "I was doing Eka Pada Sirsasana." I paused, pretty sure I'd just murdered the proper way of saying it, then went on, "It's the pose where you put your feet behind your head."

Blaze turned back from signing some paperwork Jeff handed him. "I've seen it, but I just call it the 'tryin' to lick your rear like a dog' pose," he drawled.

Misty laughed, her cotton-candy pink hair bright in the hot sun that poured through the frosted windows. Her pale green eyes danced. "It's good that you see things in poses," she told Blaze. "It suggests an open mind and gentle spirit."

Staring at her, I tried to figure out why she was complimenting him, but gave up a moment later. I was just glad she was by my side.

"You were doing, this ... this pose." Blaze's lips twitched. "And you got turned around. What does that mean?"

"I got stuck," I told him, flushing. "My hip locked up, and I couldn't move, so I had my talking home assistant thingy call Misty to come help. You can check it if you want."

"I'll be doing that. So, she came over and helped you out of your pose. How long did that take?"

"Almost an hour," Misty replied. "It took quite a while to loosen her muscles up, and since the problem was most likely caused by dehydration, I made her drink a smoothie. We talked for a good hour before I went home. I think it was around two when I left."

Blaze nodded, seeming to accept her explanation. He was even starting to look halfway nice before Jeff, who was also the town's vet, since we didn't get too many murders in the bustling county of less than 800, came back into the dining area and whispered something in his ear. Nodding, Blaze stood. Misty followed suit, her pink hair swept up in an elegant messy bun that would have made me look like a homeless rat if I'd attempted it. I was hesitant to rise, remembering Blaze's cold threat to seat me, but when Misty reached down and gave my arm a firm tug, I stood.

"Thank you for your time, ladies," Blaze said, clamping his hat down over his shiny brown hair. "Misty, if I think of anything, I'll be in touch." He sent my yoga friend a winsome smile, then turned to me, his eyes cold. "As for you—don't leave town."

Stiffening, I darted around the table as he moved past us toward the door. "And why not?" I demanded, wondering why he was all smiles and charm for Misty but crabbier than, well, a crab, to me.

He glared down at the hand I'd grabbed his arm with as if I'd personally offended him, and said, after I pulled it back, "Because, Ms. Turner, I have a murder on my hands, and a lot of evidence that's pointing me in only one direction. Stay in town. I won't repeat it again. You may have an alibi, but she's also your best friend."

He strode out the door and I was left with a sick stomach, knowing my life had just been thrown into a mixing bowl with the beater set on high.

2

"Stay in town, Ms. Turner. Don't leave Ms. Turner. I'm the law, Ms. Turner," I groused to myself as I flipped pancakes on the industrial-sized griddle in my kitchen. I avoided looking at the far wall, knowing the vault hidden behind a rack of spices was empty. My recipe book had been tagged and bagged as part of the crime scene. It's not like I needed it, but still, I missed it. The vault itself and much of my store had been dusted for fingerprints, and several photos had been taken, all while Blaze breathed down my neck as he inhaled the Butter Ribbon biscuits I'd offered him, Stetson, and Jeff.

"Better not let Blaze hear you talking like that," Terri said from behind me, and I turned, watching her as she bustled into the kitchen with a stack of dirty dishes. Since Vicki's diner was, obviously, closed, I had almost double the number of customers I usually did. They were all hangry and demanding my famous buttermilk pancakes that, as boasted on the menu, were so fluffy the clouds were jealous.

"Let him," I said boldly. "He decided from the minute I

puked on his stupid boots I must be the one who did it. You'd think they're alligator leather from the way he acted."

Terri snorted as she loaded the dishes into the steaming dishwasher. Despite the fact she worked as a dispatcher at the police station, she liked to help out at the bakery whenever she could. Though I'd offered her a full-time position, she always refused, saying she liked the fast-paced job of a 9-1-1 operator. I knew the real reason she loved it was because of all the gossip she heard, and it was probably just burning Blaze's buns for her to abandon her post on emergency leave and come help me. And I said as much.

"Blaze isn't that bad," she said. "I know he can seem a bit gruff, but once you get to know him ..."

Whirling back from stacking two plates with pancakes, apple wood smoked bacon, and fresh strawberries, I glared at her. "No. There will no 'get to know him.' At all. The guy's a jerk."

"You just haven't given him a chance, yet," she argued, coming over and squirting a generous dollop of homemade whipped cream on the strawberries. "The real reason you don't like him is because you miss how it used to be around here."

Our former sheriff, Mason Rogers, never pulled me over for speeding, while Blaze had already issued me three tickets in the matter of four months. It didn't matter to him that there'd been no one else on the road—going seventy-five in a fifty-five was a no-no.

"No," I ground out as I slung more pancake batter on the griddle, "the reason I don't like him is because he pretty much accused me of murder."

Terri grabbed the plates even as Brey called out a couple of orders through the service window. "He's just doing his job, hon'."

She left me fuming as I quickly stirred the ingredients of a batch of Call Me Caramel cupcakes. I'd met Terri when I'd moved to Flamingo Springs a little over three years ago from New York, desperate for a new start, and had immediately liked the tough woman.

My fiancé had left me at the altar, handing the best man a note to give to me, which detailed a rather disgusting love affair with my maid of honor, who was also the best man's girlfriend. Not one to let a bunch of expensive food go to waste, I'd grabbed the unity candle we were supposed to light together and burned the letter, then my veil, and proceeded to have the best party of my life.

After that, I packed up and left. While I wasn't the laughing-stock of my friends and family, I was pitied, and I didn't like it. Knowing I was the woman everyone saw as the one who got jilted, left at the altar, was a terrible feeling that made me feel like I wasn't enough. As if there was something wrong with me.

So, I sold my engagement ring and bought a ticket with the money the pawn store gave me and found myself relocating to Flamingo Springs, Texas. The place had quickly grown on me, and, deciding to put my culinary school degrees to work, I bought a gutted restaurant and refurnished it with my last penny.

Life was going great, even if I did have to miss a few meals here and there to make it work out the first year before I was officially open. Although Vicki proved to be the biggest pain in the neck I'd ever had, I was still happy. Until now. False accusations of murder would kill my business (no pun intended). I could only hope it would clear up soon, and Vicki's murderer would be caught. Who knew if they would strike again? And if they did, who would be the target?

Pouring the golden batter into cupcake liners, I slid the pan into the oven, shaking my head. No. I wasn't going to let that happen. Blaze was so busy looking at me that I doubted he'd even interrogated anyone else. I wasn't going to sit around and make fondant flowers while some killer ran loose, knocking people upside the head with rolling pins. If the new sheriff of Flamingo Springs couldn't piece two and two together, then I would. And I'd start right after I closed shop for the day, which, since today was Monday, would be 3:30 p.m., and not a minute after.

"Did they really take your fingerprints, Ms. Aubrey?" Jack Parker asked as I served him and his dad, Mike, their lunch of pancakes, sausage, and fluffy scrambled eggs colored with peppers and cheese. I gave Jack a smile even as Mike scolded him, though I saw the same curiosity mirrored in everyone else's eyes as they unashamedly leaned toward me. Lacey, owner of Lacey's Beauty is You Salon, almost fell off her stool at the old-fashioned bar where she sipped a smoothie.

"Yes," I said, waggling my fingers at the eight-year-old boy to show him the ink stains. "It was pretty cool. Kind of like being in a cop show or something." I smacked nonexistent gum, and everyone laughed. "Yes sir," I said, putting on the best drawl I could manage, for though I'd been living in the South for quite a while, I had yet to pick up the accent. "You should have seen it. There I was, handcuffed to a chair, a single light shining into my face as I was interrogated, facing up to the meanest sheriff I've ever met ..."

I continued to spin my yarn, knowing that the worst thing we could do would be to dwell on the fact that a woman had been murdered right here in the midst of our small town. Even though the police had currently ruled it as an accident to keep it quiet, most everyone knew that wasn't the case since they were interrogating people.

"And I told the sheriff," I finished as I poured syrup on Jack's pancakes and gave Jeni, owner of the local jewelry store, a refill of coffee, "that he had better sit down or else I'd be seating him!"

The round of applause I'd expected to follow my exaggerated act never came, everyone seeming to have frozen in their seats. Old Jepson Ray from a town over was holding a bite of cane-syrup-slathered biscuit halfway to his mustache, Terri's hand stopped mid-reach with a napkin to hand to Lacey. Looking around, I said, "What?" Taking on a gruff voice that was a poor imitation of Blaze's, I growled, "Confess, Turner! Or I'll run you outta Dodge!"

Still, no one moved, and finally, Mike caught my eye, before looking over my shoulder, where everyone else's attention seemed to be captured. Vaguely, I recalled hearing the tiny bell on the top of the glass door tinkle about halfway through my retelling of the interrogation. Swallowing hard, I said brightly, "Lunch is on the house, Sheriff!"

I slowly turned and stared at a pair of too familiar boots, scuffed and broken in from years of wear, looking shiny from their recent washing.

"Afternoon, Sheriff," Jepson Ray called around the bite of biscuits that had finally reached his mouth. "Cracked that case yet?"

"Not yet," Blaze replied in a conversational tone, and I let my gaze wander up his jean clad legs. "I'm actually here to ask Ms. Turner a few questions." My eyes jerked up to his, and he gave me a wolf-like grin, taking off his hat. "Is now a good time?"

Darting around the counter, Terri answered before I could tell him that it was most certainly not a good time.

"Yes. Yes, it is, Blaze. She has some things that need to get on the griddle in the back." I shot her a dirty look as I stomped toward the kitchen, holding an empty platter to my side, the white and pink frilly apron I wore suddenly looking silly over my jeans and plain shirt.

Once in the kitchen, I read the orders Brey had just pinned on the line above the order counter and slapped some bacon in a pan. "What questions did you have, Sheriff?" I asked tightly, turning around to find him less than a foot away. I swallowed. "And what do you want for lunch?"

He eyed me for a long moment, then said, "Your double platter of bacon and egg biscuits with a side of hash browns, easy on the salt." He stepped back, leaning a hip against the edge of the counter as I dug the ingredients out of the fridge. "The questions can wait, just wanted to see how you're holding up, seeing as you were the one to find her and all."

The sizzle of an egg landing on the griddle was loud as I prepared his meal. "I'm fine." I reached for another egg. *Crack.* "Thank you for asking."

I saw him frown, then run a hand through his wavy hair out of the corner of my eye, the other holding his hat next to his leg. "Yeah, well, you don't seem to be."

Crack. I slammed the egg so hard on the edge of the counter I almost ended up with it on the floor, and this time when I answered, it was through gritted teeth. "I assure you, I'm fine."

He let out a sigh and came closer, resting a tanned hand on my shaking one. "Look, I get it. You gotta put on this tough act, pretend everything's okay, like you didn't find a dead body five hours ago, 'cuz you have to run a diner and bakery, be a boss and a friend. But I also know what you're feeling, and it's okay if you need to talk, or even cry about it."

Trying my best to ignore his concerned words, I grabbed my spatula and tested the sides of his eggs while I tugged my other hand away from him and used it to flip the bacon with a fork. "Thanks. How do you like your eggs?"

He eyed the griddle. "That's not enough eggs."

"Whaddya mean? You said the double. I ain't cooking for the whole department." I don't know why I was fussing, since the whole department consisted of him and Stetson, but when it came to Blaze, I rarely saw straight.

Blaze leaned so close to my ear I could smell the mint on his breath mixed with a hint of coffee, and whispered, "You will unless you want me to tell everyone what *really* happened during the 'interview'."

"Lunch for the department it is, on me. But no dessert," I sighed before turning and batting my blue eyes at him. "And for the record, I think I did a spot-on imitation of you."

He tilted back his head and laughed, the rich sound filling the kitchen, and I realized that perhaps I'd been a bit harsh on him earlier, though he probably deserved it. "You made me sound like I'm missing a front tooth, wear a straw hat, and play the banjo for barn dances on Friday nights!" The wink that followed his words had me fighting back a blush, and I hated how his flirting affected me.

Though I tried to level him with a steady look, he only chuckled before grabbing his finished plate and moving toward the dining area. I considered chucking a dishrag at his head but refrained. Blaze Martin might have thought he'd fooled me with his charm, but he couldn't be further from the truth. I knew he would do whatever he had to in order to find Vicki's killer, and since he seemed pretty stuck on the idea that the killer was me, I had to be careful. The man didn't miss much, and I knew that every word I'd said had been carefully analyzed.

Tension settled into my shoulders, and I rolled them. Seemed to me like Blaze had already closed the case and was just waiting for the necessary paperwork to clear his desk before he arrested me with a murder charge. Since he clearly wasn't going to do anything about the real killer, it was up to me, and then we'd see who had the last laugh.

3

"Inhale," Misty said in a whispery voice to her room full of yoga students, "and exhale. Now, let us repeat. Inhale, filling your lungs, your stomach, your heart, and your mind with clean air, focusing on the verse we read at the beginning of the session. 'I can do all things through Christ ...'" the class repeated the verse with her, not an easy feat since they were inhaling.

"And exhale," Misty instructed, "letting the toxins flow from your body, releasing all that tension we tend to keep stored up. All those negative feelings, those thoughts of being unable to accomplish the tasks before us—release them into the air." She gave her class a gentle smile, a strand of vibrant hair falling over one eye.

The class members stood, palms pressed together in front of their chests, one foot up, flat against the inside of the opposite thigh. "That feels good, doesn't it?" Misty asked. "Not only does yoga purify your body, Soul Yoga helps to purify and detoxify your mind as you do away with the lies of the world and focus on the truth of Christ."

She led her class through a few more moves, then released

them with some instructions. I made my way over to her as she rolled up her gray mat. The only evidence that she'd just led twenty-five women in a rigorous forty-five-minute routine was a slight sheen of sweat on her upper lip. Not bad, since most of her clients had been dripping, even though she kept her studio cool. Misty gave me a nod as she took a swig of water, her long legs accentuated by the black yoga pants and the loose green shirt she wore. When she finally took a break from her drink, she turned to me.

"I suppose you're ready to get this show on the road?" At my nod, she locked the front door and switched the sign to Closed, then headed toward the back of her studio. "Let me take a shower first. There are some Cheetos in the kitchen, if you'd like some."

While Misty ran a tight fitness ship and had helped dozens, if not hundreds of people shed unwanted weight and develop healthy lifestyles, she also believed in moderation. She preached eating an eighty percent healthy diet and lived about eighty-five percent healthy. Though she worked out almost every day and ran a successful business teaching others to do the same, she wasn't afraid to eat a bowl of ice cream on the weekends and taught that everyone should allow themselves a treat.

She was the best kind of fitness instructor, and to her, the perfect body was a healthy body. Having a six pack and razor-sharp triceps didn't make you healthy, and positive body image was something she preached daily. She offered healthy cooking classes, and her large kitchen was always stocked with the best fruits, veggies, and meats. Misty proved you could get and maintain a rocking body without living on bean sprouts and lemon water—one of the reasons she was so popular in the fitness community, both online with her blog, and in the southern half of the States.

Helping myself to a banana and a jar of yogurt she'd made

the previous week, I took my first deep breath of the day. It wasn't until after I'd served Blaze and Stetson lunch that I'd realized how bad everything really was. When I'd closed the diner and started cleaning the kitchen, my hands were shaking. If I was arrested for Vicki's murder, I'd go to prison. I'd be punished for something I didn't do, while the real killer was still out there. What scared me even more was the thought that the killer could very well be someone I knew. After all, Vicki wasn't thought of fondly by most of the shop owners in town, having let them all feel the wrath of her razor-sharp tongue. Some weren't as forgiving as others, meaning I could have served them breakfast only hours after they had killed her.

"I'm thinking we should start with Lacey," Misty said as she came into the kitchen, now clad in jeans and a ripped tie-dyed shirt. Sneakers covered her feet, and she had her spike ring on. It was a fashion statement that also doubled as a weapon, and clearly we'd been thinking the same thing, because I was carrying pepper spray in my pocket. No one was safe, not with a killer running around, and I was glad to have her with me. On top of being armed, Misty was like a weapon herself. She'd been trained in several forms of karate, judo, and some sort of Brazilian self-defense, and I'd seen what happened when she practiced on a boxing bag.

"I think so, too," I said with a nod. "She's right next door, so maybe she saw something. Something she isn't willing to tell Blaze."

Misty gave me a look as we stepped out onto the street, which, for the sake of being a tourist town that didn't see much rain, had never been blacktopped. "You really don't like him, do you?" she said, dust puffing up on her bright purple sneakers.

I rolled my eyes as we approached Lacey's, the bright sun beating down on my shoulders as the town began to quiet down a bit. Even in the peak of tourist season, Mondays were usually slow, and today was no exception. "Whatever," I groused as we stepped up onto the wooden sidewalk. I paused, staring at Vicki's shop, cordoned off by yellow tape. Even though it'd been several hours since she'd been found, Stetson's police car was still in the side alley, its tail end sticking out from between the buildings. I'd been there when they'd carried Vicki out on a stretcher, covered with a pale blue blanket. A shiver ran down my spine, freezing an errant bead of sweat in its place.

Misty opened the clear glass door and motioned for me to go first. Stepping over the thresh hold into Lacey's Beauty is You Salon, I was transported into another universe.

Texas is a beautiful state—mile after mile of rolling plains covered in wiry green grass, and if you steer clear of the big cities, there are a lot of ranches. Flamingo Springs is located in a small patch of desert surrounded by green plains, and no matter where you go in the state, there's always the same theme: cowboy hats, horseshoes, and lassoes—usually tacked to the walls in either a rustic fashion or a chic, stylish way. Even Vicki, with all her posh-posh decorations—the bright pink and green Victorian theme, and dainty lace tablecloths—had kept true to the Texan feel. The teacups had little cows and horseshoes painted on them, and there was leather mixed in with the lace.

Cowboy boots and a bandana around my throat were usually part of my attire when I waited on tables, and Misty, in all her calm and serene yoganess, had a few ranch-like knickknacks in her studio. Everybody in Flamingo Springs, and everyone in Texas, for that matter, decorated their business with some form of cowboy attire.

Except for Lacey.

Maybe it was because she'd been born and raised in Houston and just wanted to have something different from the rest of the state. Maybe it was because she wanted to escape it.

Either way, stepping into Lacey's salon made you feel like you'd been transported into France.

Tiled with cream-colored stones and filled with Paris-themed décor and dark leather chairs, the salon was both charming and relaxing. Large pots housing luscious ferns filled the corners, and a line of old keys was strung across one pale gray wall. Little replicas of the Eiffel Tower were scattered throughout the room, their dark colorings complimenting the watercolor artwork staggered across the walls.

At the moment, Lacey sat at a small wooden table, imported from France, I'm told, painting a woman's nails. I studied her as Misty moved away, exclaiming over the new selection of organic hair dye on display by the back of the store. Lacey didn't look like a killer, but then again, did a killer ever look like their profession? She was of medium stature, with platinum blond hair (her natural color, she always said) that she wore long, almost to her waist. Being a hair and nail stylist, she always had it styled in some elegant fashion, and today, she had little braids going down her head on each side that looped up in the back in a bun. Loose curls dangled around her face as she concentrated on her client's nails, laughing as she said something.

Soft jazz music played in the background, and after a few more moments of watching my suspect, I moved over by Misty. Picking up a box of hair dye, I turned it over, pretending to read the back, though I couldn't give two hoots about it. The lengths I'd have to go to in order dye my jet-black hair were a bit too much for me. Running my finger over the ingredient list, I craned my ears toward what Lacey was saying, turning my body slightly, as if I needed more light to read the box.

"Bit of a shock, you know, hearing about it," she said as she applied a top-coat to the bright orange lacquer she'd covered the woman's nails with. "Not what you were wanting for your vacation, I'm sure."

"Well," the woman said, her poorly dyed hair wobbling on the top of her head as she nodded, threatening to spill out of its tangled knot, "I just hope everything is figured out. I can't imagine how her family and friends are doing."

"What friends?" I muttered, and Misty elbowed me.

Lacey only shook her head. "We'll let your nails cure for a second, then I'll finish them up." She eyed the woman's frizzy ponytail. "If you're in town for a while, I could dye your hair if you want, or give it a new cut." She continued yakking away about the benefits of using organic hair dye, and I turned back, putting the box on the shelf, almost upending a three-foot Eiffel Tower that stood next to it.

Steadying it, I moved away, almost ready to give up on talking to Lacey, but then I turned back, running my finger over the feet of the metal sculpture. The thing had to weigh a good five pounds, and if it fell on someone, it could really hurt. I frowned. Blaze had hinted that Vicki had been killed with a rolling pin, but what if it hadn't been a rolling pin at all? What if it had been an Eiffel Tower?

Nudging Misty, I nodded at it, but she didn't seem to catch my drift. "What if she used this?" I whispered out of the side of my mouth.

Misty frowned. "What?"

"The tower, what if she used it to kill Vicki?" I hissed.

Misty rolled her eyes. "Oh, please, Aubrey. Really?"

"Ladies," Lacey called as she ran her client's credit card, "I'll be right with you." She gave us a warning look, I guess because our whispering was ruining her jazzy atmosphere. She bid the woman farewell after handing her an appointment card, having talked her into a hair session, then came toward us.

I wondered if Lacey had the strength to heft one of the towers and hit someone in the head. But, then again, she used to be a rodeo star, so maybe she was stronger than she looked.

"Looking for something particular or just browsing?" she

asked. When we replied with the standard, "Just looking to look," answer, she stood for a moment, staring at us, tapping her lower lip with a black nail that had a rhinestone moon in the middle of it.

The thing about Lacey is that even though she does her very best to pretend she's from some hotshot city like L.A. or New York, it's not hard to guess she's originally from Texas. Even though she'd lived in both of those cities for a few years, no amount of Santa Monica or Brooklyn could erase her drawl. That's the thing about accents. You can run from the place you learned it, but it's hard to hide. I still carry my New York accent, and I'm proud of it.

Still staring at us, a frown marred Lacey's face, bronze from the hours she spent lying in the sun during her weekend escapes to the city. She'd framed her gray eyes with smoky eyeliner, and they squinted a bit as she tapped a sandaled foot on the floor, her pink shirt and black jeans smelling like chemicals.

"Blaze was in here," she finally said, turning away and sitting in one of the massager chairs. "Had the nerve to ask if I dye my hair." She sniffed. "Don't know why it's so hard for y'all to understand I came out of the womb with this hair color."

Dragging the chair her client had recently occupied over in front of her, I sat on it, while Misty struck an uncomfortable-looking yoga pose on the floor, though she'd assured me many times it was good for the spine. "At least he didn't accuse you of murdering her," I groused.

"He hardly accused you," Misty cut in from her spot by my knee, pink hair brushing her cheeks. "He just asked you stay in town because you're on the suspect list." She gave me a smile. "I'm sure he said that to everyone."

"Not me," Lacey boasted, twirling a finger through a strand of what I still secretly thought to be bleached hair. "I even asked, and he told me I wasn't a suspect, so I was free to travel."

She shook her head. "I mean, look at me. Do I look like the type of person to bash someone's head in?"

To me, that phrase sounded like something a murderer would say, but I held my tongue. "Besides," she sighed, "I had a date last night. I didn't get home until well after three."

She glanced at us, making sure she had our full attention, but before she could bore us with the details about her date with some hot shot lawyer from Houston, the door crashed opened. We all turned at the commotion to see Mabel Rose, full-time Flamingo Springs resident, my occasional kitchen help when tourist season was at its busiest, and the fastest talker this side of the Rio Grande, standing in the doorway. She worked from her home as an insurance agent, a job that paid far above minimum wage, and she scheduled her own hours.

Mabel was born with a thyroid issue that left her growth severely stunted, and it wasn't until she was in her twenties that a doctor diagnosed her. From behind, she was often mistaken for a child, but what she lacked in size, she made up for in heartiness and love. Her small stature never seemed to bother her, and I considered her to be one of my dearest friends, though she had about fifteen years on me.

"Good night!" She ran toward us, hot pink toddler sneakers flashing as the glitter on them caught the sun shining through the windows. "Y'all, one of you have to tell me it isn't true! Tell me that what I heard when I bought a loaf of bread at Jesse's isn't true!"

Grief-stricken eyes searched mine, then Misty's, before moving on to Lacey, and when we all looked at our feet, unable to tell her, she let out a whimper. Mabel is probably the sweetest resident of Flamingo Springs, and even though Vicki had a distaste for her, Mabel still loved the now-deceased drama queen.

Finally looking at her, I felt something other than shock and anger go through me. I felt ... sad. Maybe I didn't like Vicki, but others did, and now she was gone, stolen away before her time. Tears dripped down Mabel's pudgy chin, her brown eyes turning red as she cried. Stomping her foot, she wiped her face with the back of her arm.

"Tell me Blaze caught whoever did it," she said.

I shook my head as Lacey moved away to answer the jingling phone.

Mabel bit her fist, blond hair curled around her shoulders. "I don't want to know," she said around it, "but I need to know. Was it painful?"

Misty took over, saying, "No. The last thing Vicki would have known was happiness as she prepared her diner for today. She was hit in the head, so from what Blaze told me, it was as quick as someone turning a light off."

At this, Mabel began sobbing, loudly, and the couple who'd just entered the salon gave her worried looks while Lacey gave her a vicious one, obviously concerned about losing business.

"Come on, Mabel." Misty pressed a hand to her shoulder, nudging her toward the door. "Let's get out of here." Leading her out onto the sidewalk, Misty and I shared a glance over her head as Mabel did her best to corral her tears. But every time she looked at the yellow caution tape surrounding Vicki's shop, flapping in the hot breeze, she'd start bawling all over again until I finally squatted down, grabbed her shoulders, and gave her a quick shake.

"Get ahold of yourself!" I quietly shouted into her face. "Coming apart on the sidewalk isn't doing anyone any favors."

Calm and unfazed, Misty gazed off into the distance, as if she were transporting herself into her studio. While she smoothed her pink hair away from her face, Mabel gave a great hiccup before standing straight, pushing my hands away. "I'm fine now," she said. "I just—I think I'm in shock."

"Understandable." I straightened, looking both ways before

crossing the street. "Let's go to my place and get a snack. Misty and I have a lot to tell you."

Mabel was, besides Misty, my favorite person, and for good reason. She'd supported me opening a diner when others told me there was no point, since Vicki was opening one. When my first day had been a flop, everyone stuffing themselves on what Vicki had baked, Mable sat herself down and proceeded to eat three of my donuts. She'd told everyone about my creations, and to this day, I truly believe it's because of her praise (and the good Lord's provident hand) that my shop was able to take off. Seeing her so distressed made my heart ache, and as soon as I got the door to my apartment unlocked, I ushered in my two friends who were standing on the step below.

Since I live above my bakery, I always have a fresh supply of goodies, and since Mabel was a frequent visitor, I always had her favorite—chocolate chip banana bread. Like Mabel, the treat was nothing fancy, nothing special to look at it, but it had a special taste that took customers back to a happy childhood memory, making them feel all warm and comforted inside.

"Why would Blaze have you as a suspect?" Mabel asked after washing a bite of bread down with some milk. "Out of everyone in town, you should be the last one he suspects." She glanced at Misty. "No offense, of course."

"None taken," came the easy reply as Misty looked around my small apartment, seeming pleased at the few changes I'd made, adding a diffuser in one corner and changing my kitchen curtain. We usually met at my place since hers was incredibly small, and she often joked about being able to stretch her legs out and not worry about hitting a wall.

"Aubrey and Vicki weren't friends," Misty said, "but the only thing between them was competition. Vicki had far bigger arguments with almost everyone else, including me."

We all sighed at that one, and I stared at a yellow kitchen wall, remembering that night. It'd been right after I'd opened my shop, when Misty was still a bit of a mystery around town, her studio having opened only a few months earlier. Vicki had done everything she could to prevent Misty from opening, insisting that if a health freak took over, no one would want to eat sweets. When no one listened to her rants, she planted raw milk in Misty's kitchen the day before Misty taught a class, and turned her in, since selling or distributing raw milk is illegal in Flamingo Springs.

Misty almost had to close her studio due to the bad reputation the situation gave her and the fines she was forced to pay. But after managing to find out who had planted the milk, she'd went to the police and turned Vicki in. Sheriff Rogers, being drunk and lazy, turned a blind eye to Vicki's wrongdoings, but the town took notice, and Misty's studio was soon overwhelmed with customers.

It wasn't the first time Vicki had pulled a stunt along those lines, nor was it the last. Then again, there was a reason most of her clientele was either non-store-owning residents or tourists —the other store owners couldn't stand her. While I couldn't prove it, I was certain she was the one who had almost outbid me on my building, as it was something she'd do.

Mabel set her cup down, jolting me back to the present. Her pudgy hands twisted my tablecloth until I wanted to smack them, but I refrained. "If Blaze won't do his job," she declared, "I say we find out who did it."

Sharing a look with Misty I said, "That's what we were doing in Lacey's shop, Mabel. We think it might have been her."

"*You* think," Misty cut in, popping a slice of carrot into her mouth. "I said no such thing."

"Whatever," I replied, rolling my eyes. "Anyway, that's why we were there. We were looking around. I think she might have used one of the Eiffel Tower things she has."

Mabel gave a thoughtful nod. "That would do the trick, wouldn't it?" she murmured.

"Guilty before tried?" Misty raised an eyebrow. "I think you two need to cool it before Blaze catches on. And didn't Lacey say she had an alibi? I'm pretty sure that's something Blaze would have looked into."

"Her alibi could have lied," I snapped, shoving some bread into my mouth. I spoke around it, angrily brushing some hair away from my face. "Lacey might be all sweet and charming, but don't think she's forgot about the time Vicki called her a blond bimbo."

"Being insulted is hardly a reason for murder," Misty reasoned, as Mabel jumped up and rummaged in my junk drawer.

"We should make a list," she said, climbing back into her chair, feet swinging beneath the table.

"What kind of list?" I asked curiously, thinking along the lines of a grocery list, which wasn't a bad idea. Last time I'd looked in the fridge, I was out of pretty much everything, including cheese, which, in my home, is a sin. I took a deep breath, enjoying the smell of lemongrass from my new diffuser.

"A suspect list," Mabel finally replied, having pried the cap off an old ink pen. "We need to write down the names of everyone Vicki had a beef with and investigate them."

"Be a couple hundred names," I said drily, and when Misty gave me a disapproving look, I added defensively, "Well, it's true, isn't it?"

She looked away, but not before muttering, "Reading Ephesians 4:29 would do you a world of good."

Her gentle rebuttal brought me up short. I knew the verse she referenced well—in fact, I had a poster of it in my bathroom next to the mirror. "*Let no corrupt communication proceed out of your mouth, but that which is good to the use of edifying, that it may minister grace unto the hearers.*" I also had a poster of it in the bakery by the old-style wall phone, though in a newer translation, one that caught even Terri's attention when she made phone calls to her friends while waiting for a loaf of bread to bake. "*Stop all your dirty talk. Say the right thing at the right time and help others by what you say.*"

"You're right," I said. "I need to cool it." Just because Vicki and I didn't get along didn't mean I had to be quite so cruel. I don't profess to be a perfect Christian, but even I knew I was out of line.

"Don't give her any ammo," Misty mouthed as she nodded at Mabel, who was furiously scribbling away on my notepad, her hand already smudged with ink, tongue between her teeth as she squinted in thought. She seemed oblivious to our silent conversation, pausing to stare off into space before quickly scrawling another name down and sliding the paper over to me.

"I think this might be a good start," she said, laying the pen on the table before resting her chin on the edge. I'd offered to keep a booster seat on it for her, but she'd declined, and not wanting to offend her, I'd dropped it.

She caught my stare and said, "Look, Aubrey, I can't say that I had the greatest feelings of affection for Vicki, but she was somebody's daughter. Somebody's friend. We have to find who did this, because if they did it once, who's to say they won't do it again?"

"And besides that," Misty added, reaching for another stalk of celery from her saucer, "we need to figure out how she got her hands on your recipe book. No one knows the code to the vault except you, and the only fingerprints found on it were yours."

"Tell me about it," I groaned, burying my face in my hands. "If I didn't have you as an alibi, Blaze would have locked me up then and there."

Mabel slid off her chair. "That settles it then. No one kills one of our fellow residents, then frames my friend. If Blaze won't take care of it, we will."

"Wait a minute!" I reached out and dragged her back before she could march herself over to the door and down the stairs. "We haven't even looked at your list yet!" She stopped, and, after making sure Mable wasn't going to run off and perform citizen arrests on people, I turned to the list. Not too terribly long. Most of the names didn't surprise me, but a few did.

"Cody Jackson? Really? I mean, Lacey I can see, and she *was* acting odd when Misty and I tried to pump her." I gave Mabel a long stare. "But Cody? Why would you think he'd want to kill Vicki?"

Mabel crossed her arms over her chest, the dramatic sigh she gave drowned out by the loud crunch to my left as Misty finished her rabbit snack before grabbing a piece of banana bread.

"*Because*," Mable said, stressing the word, "don't you remember that they used to be an item?"

"Well," Misty interjected around her food, wiping a smear of chocolate off the small flower tattoo on the underside of her wrist, "as much of an item that you can be in Flamingo Springs."

"Even so," I said, attempting to scratch a bug bite on my thigh through my jeans, "*he* dumped her! It's not like she left him. He wanted out of the relationship."

Mabel squinted at me even as she climbed back into her chair and reached for another slice of banana bread. Taking the hint, I got up and poured her another glass of milk. "He said the only reason he dumped her is because he overheard her telling her sister on the phone that she was going to leave him. He decided it would be better to act first and save face than to deal with being rejected. That's exactly something he would do, and you know it."

Holding up a hand, I was ready to refute her point, but the thing is, I couldn't. I mean, this was Cody Jackson we were talking about. He runs a dude ranch and has posters of himself riding bulls plastered on the walls in his house for crying out loud. He's cowboy tough, but he's also a snot. Not exactly someone who murders people. Then again, most murderers don't seem capable of the crime.

"Good point." I ran my finger down the list as Misty read over my shoulder, leaning over in her chair.

"I see you've placed Lacey on your list," she said. "Why?"

"Cody chose Vicki over Lacey," Mabel said, but my shriek of surprise cut off the rest of her words.

"You've got to be kidding me!" My voice rose a bit. "Lacey Baker has the hots for ... for Cody?"

Misty held up her slender hand. Wait a minute. "Mabel, how do you know all this stuff? You're not hearing it on the grapevine, that's for sure, otherwise we'd know it too."

"Yeah," I teased. "Do you tap phones?" I got up and switched on a few lamps and the dining room light, since it was getting dusky outside.

Mabel gave me an indignant look. "In case you've forgotten, I get my hair and nails done at Lacey's. Last time I was there, which," she gave me a pointed look, "was only three days ago, she seemed upset. I asked her why, and she broke down and told me that even though Vicki and Cody weren't seeing each other anymore, he won't consider going out with her, saying he needed time. She told me he's still pining over Vicki, and if Vicki would just leave, she'd have a chance. Sounds like a motive to me."

"As for Cody, I was out at his ranch probably three weeks ago helping Jeff give the kittens their shots. I noticed Cody seemed a lot crabbier than usual, so I confronted him. He said he's angry at Vicki. Thing is, I don't think he was just angry. I think he was livid."

"Probably never been dumped before," I said thoughtfully. I tapped my chin, then leveled her with a look. "Why aren't you at the station telling all this to Blaze or Stetson?"

At the mention of Flamingo Springs one and only deputy, Misty flushed a delicate pink, and I don't think it was from the heat, since my place was quite cool. Stetson was a lifelong resident of the town, and, like Blaze, owned a ranch outside of city limits. I rather liked the tall deputy, and I could see why Misty was attracted to him. Not my type, but definitely worth a second look.

"Really?" Mabel said. "You really think that either one of them would care about some gossip?"

"They might if it involves the case," Misty told her, but I shook my head.

"No, she might be right. They'd probably laugh at us. And besides that, Mabel is one of my best friends. Blaze would just think she's saying all this to make me look innocent. Which I am," I hurried to add, "but he wouldn't see it that way. I think, for now, this should stay between us."

After everyone nodded, Misty stood. "And on that, I think I'm going home. I've a few lessons to prepare, and I need to start some more kombucha." At Mabel's protest, she said, "Mabel, it's almost nine. We've been sitting here for hours trying to come up with something. It's a little too late to be heading out to solve a murder. Let's pick this back up tomorrow, okay?"

"Fine," Mabel grumbled, snatching the list from me before I could finish reading it, "but this is staying with me."

After sending her on her way with a wrapped loaf of bread and seeing Misty down the stairs, I locked the door and went around pulling the curtains shut. Then I went through the motions of tidying everything up and checked the door three more times. The thought of a murderer being on the loose made me a bit on edge, and it was quite a while before I could talk myself into going to bed. Even then, I stared at my ceiling, listening to my fan whir in the corner as it rotated.

Had Vicki left a will behind? If she hadn't, it was going to be one big mess for her family to sort out. I myself had never seen the importance of having a will, always figuring that was something you had made up when you were a grandparent, or, at the very least, a parent. That mindset changed when my accountant in Houston corrected me during our first meeting when she helped me set up my LLC. She'd stated that having a will isn't just for the elderly, it's for the young as well, and she herself had written hers out when she was only nineteen.

"If you die and don't leave a will behind," she'd told me, "how can your family access your bank account? How will they know if you intended a certain possession to be given to a specific person?"

Though I was glad she'd talked me into it, I still shuddered to think about dying. But should I die, my assets were in complete order. I'd updated it about a year ago, with Mabel inheriting the bakery, while Misty inherited whatever was in my personal bank account, along with my car. Misty also was in charge of my health should I become unable to make my own decisions. Originally, my parents had been set to inherit everything, but they were getting on in years, and I didn't want the responsibility to fall to them. It made more sense for those who lived close to me to take control, and it gave me peace of mind knowing my business would fall into good hands.

I just hoped that wouldn't have to happen for a long, long time.

IT WASN'T until I was almost asleep, and my phone read 3:45 a.m., that I realized I'd forgotten to mix up dough for tomorrow's bread. I always did it the night before, and it was a customer favorite, so I couldn't *not* have it on the menu. It's not that it had to rise much—it was letting the spices I kneaded into it infiltrate it, giving it a fragrant smell and a heavenly taste.

Rolling onto my side, I let out a deep sigh. Maybe no one would notice if I didn't make it. I closed my eyes, hands under my pillow in a prayer position. Unless the Kevly brothers came into town. They always bought almost every loaf I had, and there'd be a high price to pay if they showed up and I didn't have any. If I didn't like them so much, it wouldn't be a problem, but I did. Especially Darren.

Groaning, I sat up, swinging my feet over the edge of my bed. After finding my slippers, I padded into the bathroom and tied my hair back in a tight French braid. I was dressed in cotton pajama pants and a tank top with a sports bra underneath it, so I didn't paint the prettiest picture, but who cared? It was the middle of the night. No one was going to see me anyway.

Sleepily, I made my way down the outside stairs and unlocked the backdoor to my bakery. I was calculating how much I needed of everything and already planning the day's special as I flipped on the kitchen lights. I opened at eight o'clock on the dot, and this bread wouldn't make itself. Washing my hands, I set to work, and even though I was exhausted, I moved quickly, enjoying myself, as I always did when I was alone in the kitchen. Unlike most of the other stores in town, I don't have music playing in the background, preferring silence or the happy hum of satisfied customers as a soundtrack, and I let out a contented sigh in the soothing quiet.

Except for its base, the bread doesn't have an exact recipe, and I'd started calling it Gold Mine Loaves because of all the goodies in it. Besides bacon, jalapenos, and cheddar cheese, I was known to add a few other surprises, such as dark chocolate chunks, pepperoni, and the occasional piece of sweet pineapple. Hot or cold, it was delicious, and I always served it with a side dish of homemade strawberry jam.

Soon, the delicious smells of spices, herbs, and pickled jalapenos filled the air, and I gave my full focus to the task of buttering several metal bread pans. Hearing a soft scraping noise above the whir of the stand mixer, I turned. A tall person in a trench coat stood behind me. I reached toward the counter for my phone as they brought their arm up. Something hard connected with the side of my head, and I dropped to the floor like a sack of flour.

4

Head pounding, I slowly opened my eyes, trying to blink the grittiness out of them. Seeing a concerned face peering down at me, I let out a scream.

"Aaahh!" I sat straight up, shoving at Blaze as I tried to scramble away, lunging straight into a cabinet.

"Whoa," Blaze grabbed my ankle and pulled me back. "It's just me."

Rolling over from my snake position on the floor after admiring how clean the grout between the tiles was, I eyed him. He'd been squatting over me, balanced on the toes of his boots, and when I'd shoved him, he'd fallen backwards onto his behind. Even in his awkward position, he looked ready to save the town from evil, and once it finally registered in my brain that it really was Blaze and not my attacker, I lunged again, this time at him.

"Blaze, s-s-someone tried to kill me." I said the words as calmly as I could, a feat I'm rather proud of, because it wasn't easy since I was saying it into his chest. I'd moved toward him for protection, not sure how long I'd been out, but I'd somehow ended up in his lap, like I was using him as a human shield.

"No kidding?" he said, the words rumbling through his chest, and I nodded, his tan button up shirt soft against my cheek and smelling of cologne, leather, and gun oil. My head pounded, and I was aware of aches and pains in my legs and arms. "Can you give me a time?" he asked, and it was then that I became very aware of the fact he had one arm around me, hand splayed on my back.

"4:30. Ish." I said, and he chuckled.

"It's after six now, so I think you're safe." In other words, *'Get off me.'*

Letting his arm drop as I pulled away from his chest, he mimicked his other hand as he braced it on the floor, leaning back. That's when the dizziness hit me.

"I don't feel so good," I said, reaching up to clutch my head. As soon as my fingers made contact with the right side of my head, I found out why. An egg size lump jutted out from it, and when I pulled my hand away, it was sticky with blood.

Blaze was studying me, and I realized I was still in his lap, but my head was hurting too much to really process anything but the pain. It took all I had to slide off him to the floor. "My head hurts."

"I wonder why," he said dryly, and this time when he reached out after switching back to a squat, I let him. His breath was warm as it fanned against my cheek, and I flinched when he probed my wound. "Don't think you'll need stitches," he said. "Probably have a concussion. I'll get Doc down here to take a look at you. Or," here, he gave me a hard look, "I can take you to the clinic."

I started to shake my head, thought better of it, and said, "I can't leave the diner. I've got to get muffins going. I open in less than an hour. I don't have time for this." I struggled to my feet, grabbing onto the edge of a counter for support, but before I'd even managed to straighten, the floor tilted, and I crashed back down and into Blaze, who let out a grunt as his feet shot out in front of him. He landed on his back with my not-so-light carcass sprawled, once again, across his chest, the handle of his pistol thudding against the tile.

The rest of his utility belt dug into my stomach, and I tried to push away from him, placing my hands on his firm chest. With a growl and I think a smothered curse word, he wrapped his arms around my back and held me in place. "Now look here," he bit out, hat half falling off his head as he glared up at me, "someone about bashed your brains out this morning. Don't try to finish what they left undone!"

Staring at him, I realized in my slightly delirious state that the sheriff wasn't a bad-looking man. In fact, to be very honest, he was rather attractive. Even when he wasn't smiling, like right now, he had dimples that slashed into his tan cheeks, and his eyes were the most unusual green I'd ever seen, sort of like the shade of an ocean-smoothed piece of glass. His chin was firm and strong, a small scar on the bottom of it, and he had a jaw you could slice cheese on.

I mentally shook myself. I needed some ice for my head, maybe then I could think straight. "Let me up," I grunted at him, pushing on his chest, but even though he had my dead weight crushing his ribcage, Blaze's arms were like bands of steer rope. They gave a little, then held, and at the moment, I was struggling to remember why I disliked him so much.

Our eyes met, and he said, "I'm going to let go now, Aubrey, and when I do, you are going to slowly, and very carefully, sit up and lean against the cupboard, okay?" He said it softly, but there was no missing the authority in his voice. I gave him a tiny nod, which I immediately regretted, as it sent pain ricocheting down my neck.

He loosened his arms, and I sat up. He followed suit, so that we were nose to nose, most of my weight on his legs. "I swear, Aubrey, you try and pull that stunt again, I'll tase you and drag your sorry rear to Doc's, bakery or no bakery. Got it?"

Without waiting for me to answer, he gripped my upper arms and moved me to the floor, and once I was pressed against a cupboard, he stood and rummaged through my freezer. Finding a bag of ice, he handed it to me along with a dishtowel. Pulling his phone from his belt, he dialed a number and spoke with someone—Jeff, most likely—then started looking the kitchen over.

After watching him dig through the fourth drawer I snapped, "What? Looking for the rolling pin you're sure I hit myself with?" The words came out way sharper than I had intended, and in an instant, Blaze went from concerned to annoyed. But instead of letting his scowl back me down, it only raised my hackles even more, and I added, "I mean, after all, I did Vicki in, so I needed to make myself look innocent, right? Gotta bash myself in the head so I'm off the suspect list—just like in the movies."

It was the last line that set him off, and the next thing I knew, he was bent over me, once again in my face, a favorite tactic of his, I decided. "Any of this look like a movie to you?" he snarled at me, gesturing at a smeared pool of blood a few feet away that I hadn't noticed. "You think someone getting murdered, then the same thing almost happening to you is a joke?" He snorted as I blinked at him. "I can't believe you're that self-centered. Oh, wait, yes I can." He stood and went to let Jeff in, saying over his shoulder, "Aubrey, if I thought you murdered Vicki, I'd have you sitting in jail awaiting trial."

Blaze's words weren't really that harsh, nor was his tone, but when you're sitting on the floor of your bakery kitchen with blood oozing down the side of your face from someone attempting to kill you after they succeeded in murdering your rival the day before, and a super-hot sheriff is chewing you out, your emotions get a bit confused. As in, I should have given Blaze's attitude right back, but instead, I started bawling. Like, really bawling, with big tears streaming down my cheeks, and my face all screwed up in a frown.

"Take a chill pill, huh, Blaze?" Doc Peterson, or, Jeff, as most everyone knew him, said as he knelt next to me and rummaged through his leather bag for gloves. Yes, Flamingo Springs' one and only doctor and vet does house calls, and yes, he carries around a medical bag that was probably used in the Civil War. I always teased him about it, but for once, I couldn't find a joke anywhere in my throbbing head. All I could do was stare at him as I cried.

"Hey, now," he said, gently smoothing my frizzy hair away from my face while Blaze looked on with a glare, "let's take a look at your head." He sucked on a tooth as he probed at my wound before diving back into his bag. "Wanna tell me why you're crying?" He came back up with a penlight and shined it at my head, then into my eyes before giving me a basic reflex check.

Had anyone but Jeff asked, I would have blown them off, because the only person I tell my deep dark secrets to is the Lord. But I liked Jeff. He couldn't have been more than thirty-five, but he's the kind of guy you *want* to tell everything to, because you know he actually cares. He's like a big teddy bear, and all I've ever felt around him is comfortable. Momentarily forgetting that Blaze was still present, I started blubbering on Jeff's shoulder as he patted my back.

"My head hurts, my butt hurts from hitting the floor, my bread is ruined, I don't know how I'm going to open today, and Blaze saw me in my pajamas!" Though Blaze and my attire had made the final part of my tirade, I ended my speech by letting out a big sob, even as the aforementioned jerk of a sheriff started chuckling.

"Well," Jeff said, easing me back so he could clean my wound, "those are some pretty good reasons to cry." He gave me a wink before leaning back in to coat my head with antiseptic, which made me flinch. "And besides, what's so bad about your pajamas? They're pretty cute."

The last bit got a smile out of me. Keeping up a steady patter of both gossip and legit news, Jeff had me patched up in only a few minutes, declaring I didn't need stitches and only had a slight concussion. He gave me a small bottle of pain killers, a packet of salve for my head, and verbal instructions on how to clean my wound.

By then, Blaze had finished mopping the blood off the floor and was checking the back door. "No sign of forced entry," he said as Jeff left after helping me into a chair he'd grabbed from the closet and unfolded. "Looks like they used a key."

Propping my head up with one hand as I rested my elbow on the counter, I held up the other. "I'm the only one with a key to the backdoor, and I always lock it behind me. The front door uses a different one, and the only person besides me to have a key for it is Brey."

Blaze leaned against the counter next to me, snapping the emergency ice packet Jeff had given me until it crackled and started freezing. The bag of ice from earlier was sitting in the industrial sized sink, its plastic outside stained a streaky red. He handed me the packet and waited until I had it pressed against my bandaged head before speaking.

"I'm sorry for making you cry," he said, meeting my eyes, his own serious. "I was out of line." He gave me a grin that bordered on being sheepish, eyes crinkling at the corners.

Studying him, I debated on how to respond to his unexpected apology—my lack of trust in men cautioning me to be careful. He cut a fine figure leaning against the counter, cowboy hat pushed back, one hand resting on the butt of his pistol. His shirt was stained with dried blood, and he had a few spots on his Wranglers, though he'd managed to keep his boots clean. A strand of glossy brown hair had escaped from under his hat and laid across his forehead. My stomach fluttered.

After a moment, he went on, "I gathered what evidence I could, which was none, so I think the next step is for you to call Mabel and have her run the diner today." He gave me a stern look. "I'll wait around till she gets here, then I want you to get a shower and relax. Maybe get something to eat."

"I can't." Slight panic colored my words. "The Kevly brothers should be stopping by today, and they'll be expecting Gold Mine Loaves. I have to start all over."

Blaze held up a hand, then jerked a thumb at the counter across the kitchen. "Looks to me like you got about eight loaves finished before your friend showed up," he said, and looking at the counter by the stove, I saw that he was right. Eight neat loaves were lined up on cooling racks, but I had no memory of baking them, only mixing them, and I told him so.

He shrugged. "You got whacked in the head, Aubrey. You probably just don't remember baking them."

"No," I said slowly, "I hadn't been down here forty-five minutes before ..." I paused and swallowed hard. At his nod, I went on, "Even if I had put the bread on to bake, there's no way I would have had time to pull it out of the oven." I shifted the ice on my head, wincing when the fridge kicked in, the low rumble sending waves of pain through my teeth. "Do me a favor and go feel a loaf."

Blaze gave me a dubious look, but he must have sensed I was on to something, because he went across the kitchen and touched the back of his wrist to a loaf. "They're still pretty warm," he said, obviously confused. He opened the oven and stuck his hand inside. "And the oven is still hot."

Giving my kitchen a good look, my eyes finally deciding to focus, I noticed that my mixer was back in its corner. The base had been wiped down, the mixing bowl and bread hook clean and locked in place. "Did I get hit in the head, get back up, and do all this?" I asked, wondering if sleepwalking while suffering a head wound was possible.

Blaze narrowed his eyes. "There would be blood every-where if you did." He crossed back over by me, and thin lines fanned out around his mouth. He had a strange look in his eyes and was obviously troubled. "Aubrey, whoever tried to kill you thought they had. And then they stuck around and finished baking the bread and cleaning the kitchen."

He gave me a hard look, his mind obviously trying to get an angle on what I knew to be a rather unusual scene. "The recipe for your bread, is it in your book or is it one that's common?"

"Common," I answered, puzzled, staring at a black skid mark on the floor, wondering where it had come from, since I was in slippers and Blaze was wearing boots. "But why would they do that? And why would they think I was dead? I was still breathing!"

"Barely," he told me. "I thought you were dead when I came in." At my raised eyebrows as I laid the ice pack on the counter, he added, "I just got this gut feeling that something was wrong, and when I tried your back door, it was unlocked. I couldn't tell if you were breathing or not even when I was right next to you, and when I felt for a pulse, I almost couldn't find it."

My mouth suddenly felt dry. I met his eyes again. "What kind of person bakes bread while someone is dying on the floor?"

Blaze looked grim as he reached for his phone and called Stetson. "I don't know, but this case just got a lot weirder."

5

"Five, six, seven, eight, and bounce!" I held the phone away from my ear as Mabel shouted, "Hold on, Aubrey!" The jazzy music of an exercise video in the background cut out, and then she came back on the line, breathing hard. "What's up?"

Blinking away images of her clad in workout clothes colored a distinctive pink hue made popular nausea medicines complete with '80s-style sweatbands, I cleared my throat. "Someone attacked me this morning. Probably the same person who killed Vicki." I went on over her gasp, "I know this is short notice, but could you run the diner today? It's Terri's day off, and she'll be here in about an hour."

My eyes moved from the floor to Blaze's back as he talked with Stetson, who was changing my back lock, since Blaze had decided to believe me about always locking it. As if feeling my eyes on him, Blaze turned and looked at me. I let my gaze drop away. Maybe it was from being hit in the head, maybe it was because I was sitting in my kitchen wearing slippers and cartoon pajamas while two hunky cowboys were at my beck and call, but I was more than a little flustered. My cheeks felt hot while I focused on what Mabel was currently shrieking in my ear, even as my gaze was drawn back to the strange scuff marks on the floor.

"Thank God you're okay." She paused to pant. "Just let me shower and I'll be over in about twenty minutes, okay? You just worry about getting better and figuring out who did this."

"Uh, Mabel?" I cautioned, since there was no way she could shower and make the drive to town in under twenty minutes without breaking a few laws. "Don't speed." I eyed Blaze. I considered him to be ticket happy, and despite the situation, I had no doubt he would fine Mabel for speeding.

"Let me worry about Blaze," she chuckled into my ear before hanging up. "That boy should just try and ticket me!"

Blaze let out a laugh as I ended the call. I looked up to see that Stetson was gone. It was just me and the sheriff again. At my raised eyebrow he grinned. "Like Mabel's car could go past thirty-five! I can crawl faster than that car with the pedal pushed through the floorboard."

Smirking, I moved toward the back door to head up to my apartment. Being such a small person did come with a set of problems, many of which Mabel brushed off as if they were no more than gnats, but driving a car was one that had stumped her for years. That is, until she'd discovered smart cars. Less than a day after seeing an infomercial, she became the brand-new owner of one, and since she believed in going all in for everything she did, she had it custom painted. Choosing red and yellow, it resembled one of those primary-colored plastic ride-on cars for kids and got more than a few laughs from tourists.

"Do you need anything else?" I asked, one hand resting on the newly changed doorknob, the other pressing the ice pack to my head, the new key in my pocket.

Blaze shook his head, tucking a little book he'd been taking notes in back into his stained shirt pocket. "Nah, you're good.

I've got your statement, processed the crime scene, did everything I can do. You go on up and take it easy." He gave me a hard look. "Let Mabel and Terri handle the crowd today, and be sure to call Misty."

He started to turn away and I stepped outside, but then paused. "Blaze?" When he turned around, I went on, "Am I still on your suspect list?"

He stared at me, pulling in one corner of his mouth like he was contemplating saying something, and I had to force myself to stop admiring the way his lashes framed his brilliant eyes. Finally, he said, "Until I've got someone in jail, everyone is on the suspect list, including you."

After giving him a careful nod, I closed the door and went up to my apartment, frustrated and more than a little embarrassed. On one hand, like any innocent suspect, I was ticked that he didn't believe me. On the other hand, I knew he was just doing his job, and that just because someone had taken a whack at me didn't mean I hadn't killed Vicki.

From the day he'd been transferred in as the new sheriff, Blaze and I had butted heads. When he'd went around issuing citations for stupid stuff like double parking and disturbing the peace with loud music, I'd followed behind, giving out free cupcakes to soothe the burn he'd caused. I'd even stopped in his office a few weeks after he'd been sworn in, offering up some advice about taking it easy on the residents. It wasn't well received, and after giving me a glare so cold it knocked the outside temperature down a few degrees, he'd escorted me out. Of course, the comment I'd made about his name being better fitted for a horse hadn't exactly helped my case.

No one liked him. At least, not at first, but after he started a search for Jack Parker's dog and found the ungrateful beast two days later, he suddenly became everyone's favorite person. Except for mine. I kicked a slipper into the corner. Maybe one day that would change—if he'd stop giving me tickets. But for now, it looked like I was still on the case to find out who the Flamingo Springs' murderer was.

STEPPING INTO LACEY'S SALON, I let my eyes adjust before moving forward. I'd called her earlier, after getting out of the shower, scheduling an appointment to have my nails done. I needed the relaxation, I'd told her, after my harrowing experience that morning. It was now 11:00 a.m., a mere five hours after Blaze had found me on the floor, and I was no closer to figuring out who had tried to kill me.

Mabel and Terri were running the diner, and doing a good job of it, too. Once the Kevly brothers had eaten their fill of pancakes and strawberries and had bought most of my Gold Mine Loaves, they'd been on their way, though not before Darren had asked me out to a movie on Friday in Houston. Of course, I'd said yes amid Mabel's muffled squeals in the kitchen, only to remember I wasn't allowed to leave town, so we'd settled on going to Cody's ranch together for the Fourth of July celebration.

Lacey looked up from counting her till and gave me what I call her Texas smile. Lacey is one of the prettiest women I've ever met, and her smile is like a thousand-watt light bulb. It stretches across her face, and pulls her eyes into it, lighting them up, and it's so big and so genuine, that I started calling it her Texas smile.

"How's the head?" she asked, shutting the drawer with her hip and moving around the counter. "I heard you gave Blaze quite the scare."

Touching my head, I gave her a grimace. I'd left my shoulder length hair down and brushed over one shoulder so that it wasn't pressing on the wound, and though I was doped up on enough painkillers for a horse, I still had a headache. "It's okay," I said. "Apparently, I've got a hard head and an even harder will to live."

Plopping down in the chair she ushered me over to, I stuck my hands out to her as she took her seat. Soft music played in the background, and I closed my eyes as she cleaned my nails and conditioned them, her voice soothing as she talked. "I'm honestly getting scared to be by myself when it's dark," she confessed. "I mean, first Vicki, then they tried to get you." I could almost hear her shrug. "I always thought Flamingo Springs was a great place. Obviously, since I came back to start a business, but now, I'm not so sure."

Cracking open an eye as she slathered a peel off base coat onto my nails, I stared at her. "What do you mean 'they'? You think it's the same person?"

She lifted one shoulder, strands of curled platinum hair teasing her cheeks even as feather earrings brushed her jaw. "I mean, don't you think so, Aubrey?" She swiped at my thumb. "It's really starting to freak me out."

Toes crossed in my sandals since she could obviously see my fingers, I cleared my throat." Blaze said these cases might be unrelated." I giggled when she massaged my hands, waiting for the base coat to dry. She worked her way up to my wrists before responding, shaking her head.

"I don't know. I mean, maybe? But you know what I think?" She stopped massaging the underside of my wrist and looked me in the eyes, the troubled look in her gray ones highlighted by the heavy black eyeliner she wore. "I think we have a beginning serial killer on our hands, and if Blaze and Stetson don't figure out who it is soon, they're going to strike again. They almost got you. What if they try again? What if they move on to someone else who doesn't have your concrete skull?"

For some reason, her words, though stated matter-of-factly and with a drawl, sent a shiver straight up my arms and down my back. I looked away from her, past her shoulder and at the brick wall, chewing on my bottom lip. It was a few moments before my brain registered what my eyes were seeing, and when it did, my mouth went dry. And it wasn't from the sharp smell of the turquoise-blue polish Lacey was painting onto my fingertips.

The Eiffel Tower I'd pointed out to Misty only the day before was still on the shelf, but now it had a good-sized dent in it—about the size of the side of my head. I swallowed hard. Not an easy feat when you've got no spit left in your mouth. I looked back at Lacey, who was bent back over my nails, muttering something about the benefits of the polish she was using, then back at the decoration.

My eyes darted back and forth at least three times before I finally realized that I could very well be getting my nails done by the same person who had tried to kill me. I gave myself a slight shake. Who was I kidding? This was Lacey I was thinking about! Now that yesterday's adrenaline had worn off, clearing my mind, I knew there is no way on this green earth that she's capable of murder. Petty? Yes. Able to rope a bull and beat out all the competition? Most certainly.

But capable of murder? I couldn't see it. No matter how hard I tried, I simply could not see Lacey hurting anyone, not even Vicki. And the good Lord in all His knowledge knows those two have gone at it a time or two.

Staring at the blond head draped in loose braids and curls bent over my hands, I watched as she artfully drew multicolored feathers in the middle of my very blue nails, gluing a tiny pink rhinestone at the base of each one. Her slender shoulders, tanned and strong with a slight dip in the top of each one, were sprinkled with a few faint freckles, and her sequin covered sleeveless blouse and glittered sprayed jeans did everything but scream girly. They did not scream murderer.

The muscles in Lacey's slim arms rippled as she twisted the lid off the bottle of a clear topcoat, and I took back my last thought. "What?" she asked, catching my glance, and figuring if she wanted me dead bad enough, she'd find a way no matter what. I let out a gusty breath.

"What happened to your Eiffel Tower?" I pointed at it with a ritzy nail, and she twisted around to look.

"Funny thing," she said, still opening the nail polish. "I came in this morning, and it was on the floor along with a couple bottles of dye, two of which had busted open." She turned back to face me while I struggled to school my expression. "The window had been forced open, and it looked someone had tried to get in the till. Stetson came by and found some shoe prints beneath the window, about a size ten, but because they were so faint, he figured it was a kid looking for a thrill. Of course, he decided that after he asked to see the bottom of my shoe to make sure I don't wear that size. He had the nerve to think I wear a size ten. No, honey, I'm a size seven and a half." A loud huff filled the room. "Like I have time to break into my own store. He mumbled something about insurance fraud, but if that was what my intention was, don't you think I would have done a bit more damage?" She frowned. "I get my hands whoever did it, they're gonna wish they'd broke into someone else's store."

She finished my nails. "One of the dye bottles leaked all over it, and I spent an hour scrubbing red dye off that thing. I mean, it cost me a fortune, so I couldn't throw it away, and since it was temporary hair dye, it came off, for the most part."

"What about the dent?" I asked, my heart pounding so hard I thought it was about to pop right out of my chest onto the table, because I was pretty sure the dye was only there to cover up the blood from my head.

Lacey bit her lip, scratching her wrist. "Yeah, that's the weird part. Maybe whoever broke in got mad they couldn't get into the till, so they decided to break some of my stuff." She gave me a stern look. "I'm not supposed to tell anyone about this, so please don't say anything."

After I agreed, she stood, and I followed her to the counter where she rang up my manicure and swiped my card. "I almost didn't open today since I spent the night in Houston with Gemmi. Remember her?" She went on without waiting for an answer, "But then Tod canceled our picnic today because he had some sort of emergency meeting with a client for a trial next week, so I went ahead and came back." She cocked her head as she gave me a receipt. "I don't eat out much, but I was starving, so I stopped at this little truck-stop diner on the way here, probably at five-thirty or so." She shuddered. "They could use a few lessons from you."

"For that, next time you come over, the pancakes are on me." My diner was best known for its cupcakes and pancakes, and I'm not lying when I say that I have the best muffins in the southern half of the states. If I'm being honest, I probably have the best food in the entire United States. Or the world, for that matter.

Squinting at her, I tucked my credit card into my wallet, then slung my purse over my shoulder. "Because I'm nosy, what was the name of the diner?"

Lacey tapped a neat nail on the countertop, thinking. "Something cowboyish, like Dave's Taters or something." She ran her finger down her appointment book, checking the clock on the wall behind me, then snapped her fingers. "Dave's Taters, Steakers, and Gators, that's what it was!"

"Steakers?" I asked, and she snickered.

"It rhymes with Taters, so I think that's why he used it, and as for the gator part ..." She gagged. "He serves alligator, and trust me, you do *not* want to try the gator hash." She grimaced. "It was like chewing out the hind end of a pole cat."

Chuckling, I moved toward the door, mentally tucking away the name of the diner to double check her alibi later that day.

Thanking her one last time before leaving, I headed over to Jesse's Grocery Mart, which was down the street, one building from the end of town. The thing about Flamingo Springs is that while the county boasts a population of eight hundred, it's a scattered eight hundred. You can stand at one end of town, look down its single street and see the desert on the other side. Almost everyone who owns a business lives above it, except for Vincent and Maria, who own Esposito's, and Blaze and Stetson, who all live on ranches a few miles from town. In total, about sixty people actually live in the city limits, everyone else is spread out over a fifty-mile radius, most of whom just drive past to Houston unless they want their nails done.

It'd been an adjustment, moving from New York City to such a small, set-back place. Now, as I pushed open the grocery mart's glass door and stepped into soothing coolness, I loved it, and I don't think I could go back to the busyness of a big city.

"Aubrey!" Jesse greeted me as he rang up a cartful of groceries for Jaime Knights. "What's cookin' good lookin?" Eighties rock music played over the sound system, almost drowned out by the whir of the fridges lined against the back wall. He'd started decorating for the Fourth of July, stringing red, white, and blue banners everywhere, streamers hanging from the ceiling. You can see pretty much the entire store from the entrance, and it looked like Jaime and I were his only customers, noon being a dead hour for most places in town.

Shaking my head as I grinned, I grabbed a basket. Jesse was probably the happiest guy in town and a confirmed bachelor. 'Once married, once divorced, and never doing either again,' was his motto, and you could count on him to special order whatever you wanted, even if it was lobster, something Lacey had the habit of eating every Friday. He'd even set up an isle for special orders, something that had endeared him to pretty much everyone in town.

"Doing okay, hon?" Jamie asked after smacking the hand of

her three-year-old son, Andy, when he tried to grab a candy bar from the stand by the register. "Heard you took a nasty hit to the head this morning."

Shoulders lifting in a shrug, I smiled at her. "It hurts, but I think it'll be all right in a few days. How's life?"

"Oh," she laughed as she took a bag from Jesse and put it in her cart, "same old, same old. Nothing exciting happening at my household except for the realization that since Cynthia starts Algebra this fall, I need to actually learn how to do it myself. Rob is too busy this go around." She grinned before leaning down and delivering another solid blow to Andy's hand.

He gave her a baleful look before sticking out his lower lip and crossing his arms over his chest. She ignored him and continued talking, speaking up over the beep of Jesse's barcode scanner. "And besides Rob buying a new horse, we pretty much do the same thing day in and day out. The only break is when we come to church on Sundays."

She turned and dug in her purse, not noticing the piece of candy Jesse slipped Andy. As she came up with a handful of coupons, I moved a few feet away, placing some boxed noodles and a container of salt in my basket. Jaime was a mom of six kids, and she homeschooled all of them. The oldest was sixteen, the youngest being Andy, and between that and helping her husband around the ranch and making a successful living of selling designer clothing, she had little time for anything else. I did less than half of what she did, and I never looked as put together.

Part of her clothes-selling business was displaying it wherever she went, so Jaime was always decked out in a pair of uniquely designed tights, usually a solid-colored blouse, and a long jacket. The one time I'd looked at buying some of her merchandise left me more than a little confused, as all the clothing had names, like 'Sarah,' or 'Mary.' Made no sense to me, and I decided I'd stick to jeans and T-shirts.

Jaime could be pushy with her products, and it'd taken her quite a while to warm up to me after I'd turned down her offer of a house party. I knew her name was on Mabel's suspect list, which was currently sitting on my kitchen table, Mabel having been kind enough to email me a copy. Her reasoning for Jaime to have a motive for murder was that Vicki had decided to start selling the same clothing brand as well, wearing and displaying it in her shop, which took away a good portion of Jamie's clientele. Jaime and Rob needed every penny they could get with raising six kids, and with Vicki gone now, Jaime would stand to make a lot more money.

However, I couldn't see how she'd find the time to murder Vicki, but nonetheless, I eyed her. She practically touched her chin to Jesse's hand to make sure he was correctly entering every coupon while Andy clung to the bars of the cart like a jailed convict, running his nose across them.

Clearly I wasn't the only person wondering if she'd gotten Vicki's customers because Jesse said, entering another coupon, "You know, I still can't believe Vicki's gone. Think you'll get her business?"

Jesse's tone was innocent, his eyes on his screen, but he might as well have pointed a finger and accused Jaime of murder because she straightened. From my position to the side of her where I was grabbing a head of lettuce from a cooler, I could see her nostrils flaring as her cheeks took on a hue almost as red as her dyed hair. Even Andy cowered away, sensing that his mother was about to explode.

Jamie pointed at Jesse's name tag, her French tipped finger shaking, toes curled in her flip-flops, and in her hot green tights, yellow blouse, and blue cardigan, she looked like an avenging parrot. "You see that tag?" she asked, her voice tight, and looking down, Jesse nodded.

"Yes, ma'am, I sure do. Put it there myself this morning." His lips twitched.

Jaime tapped it. "It's says 'grocery mart manager,' not 'sheriff,' so I think you need to keep your snide comments and questions to yourself!" She jammed her credit card into the chip reader so hard it started to bend, and I thought it'd snap in two. I could hear her angry pants even as I moved out of her sight and worked my way to the back of the store. The sudden lack of conversation was almost deafening, the sound of Jesse ripping her receipt off the machine painfully loud.

Jamie's flip-flops slapped across the floor, and I heard her ram the door open with her cart, growling a threat at Andy, who apparently wasn't moving fast enough. Grabbing a box of crackers, I peeked around the edge of the isle and watched her stomp to her van and jerk the side door open. Andy, having caught on that his mother was in the mood of all moods, dove headfirst into his car seat, barely avoiding a gallon of bleach to the head.

Cranking the van to life, she revved it a few times, staring through the glass doors at Jesse, almost like she was going to ram the building, then roared away, leaving her cart in the street. After she'd gone, Jesse turned and caught my eye as I peered around a display of crackers. He chuckled. "She'll probably call Blaze and tell him I was harassing her." He smoothed back his short blond hair before straightening his dark green apron. "It's not like I'm the first person to suggest it, and I won't be the last." He grabbed a few paper sacks and opened them, flattening the bottom for the next customer. "Besides, I needed some entertainment."

Sure that if Jaime had been planning on making the store a drive-thru she would have done so by now, I came the rest of the way around the corner. "I think being accused of murder would be pretty offensive," I told him as I started laying items on the conveyer belt. "I mean, Jaime murdering Vicki? I heard you have to swear some sort of oath to sell those clothes. Wouldn't that go against it?"

Jesse laughed at me as he started scanning my groceries, the lights dimming for a moment as a freezer kicked in. "I think it's waived if it makes you a top consultant."

Grinning at each other, we both knew he'd hear no end to what had just happened, but as he scanned item after item and placed them into paper bags, my mind started working. Jaime had said something about Jesse not being the sheriff, and it had sounded to me like Blaze had already seen that she would have had a motive to kill Vicki and had followed up on it. I scowled. I just wished he was a little more laid back, because then, maybe he could share his theories and I wouldn't have to chase after every suspicious person in town.

"The funeral's Thursday," Jesse said quietly, interrupting my criminal investigator mindset. I looked at him as he tapped out a code on his screen, taking in his pressed gray slacks and the rolled-up sleeves of his white dress shirt. He suddenly seemed sad, and then I remembered that at one point, he and Vicki had dated, though it hadn't lasted more than a month before she'd dropped him.

Catching my sympathetic gaze, he tried to muster up a smile. "Maybe her and I didn't have anything, and maybe she was a bit of a cactus, but why would someone kill her?" He swallowed. "I just hope she knew where she was going after death."

Opening my mouth, I was ready to offer up a lame phrase of comfort, but I hesitated. I sent up a silent prayer and reached out, touching his arm. "Look, I didn't get along with her either, but just because we couldn't always see the good in her doesn't mean she was bad. God determines what's in our hearts, and He makes the decision of where we go." I let out a laugh that turned into a sigh biting my lip before continuing. "And that's a good thing, because if we made that decision,

I'm pretty sure Jaime would have you in a hot place right now."

When Jesse finally met my gaze I went on, "I think that deep down, Vicki was an amazing woman, and I think she had a love for God."

He nodded and gave me my total. As I scrounged around in my purse for my wallet, he said, "I hope Blaze gets whoever did it, and whoever hurt you! If I find out who it was ..." he let his words trail off and cracked his knuckles, and I smiled. Jesse isn't a super big guy, but like most men of the region, he knows his way around with a gun and a rope, and hog tying is second nature.

After talking for a few more minutes, I made my way home, where I put away my purchases. I then ate a light lunch and opted for a nap, hearing the happy hum of satisfied customers echo up through my floorboards as they feasted on pancakes, cupcakes, crispy bacon, and fresh bread. Terri and Mabel's laughs occasionally rang out as they joked, the clatter of pots and pans a comforting sound.

Misty had promised to come over after her last class was finished, and I hadn't heard from her since. Then again, she had back-to-back appointments all day, one of them with a rather famous and wealthy client, so I wasn't surprised.

Stretching out on my leather couch, I stared at the off-white ceiling, basking in the light breeze the ceiling fan sent over me. As my eyelids dropped, I realized that there was another person we needed to add to our list. Jesse had been bummed when Vicki had left him, and just like with Cody, it was a motive for murder. News reports always said that the first place officers looked was at the significant other of the victim. And at the exes. Jesse was an ex, and even though I didn't like the idea, I knew I had to follow up with him, because he very well could be the murderer.

HOLDING UP A FINGER, I silenced Misty and Mabel as they fought over the last Dorito in the bowl, Terri and Brey now running the diner. "It's ringing," I hissed. "Shut up!"

Misty gave me her signature frosty look, green eyes daring me to make her hush while Mabel stuck her tongue out at me, but I turned my attention away from them as they started a game of rock, paper, scissors. I choked a bit when a man answered the phone. "Dave's Taters, Steakers, and Gators, what can I grill for ya?"

"Yeah, uh," I cleared my throat, taking on a heavy drawl that somewhat mimicked Lacey's while Misty and Mabel made fun of me. "Is this Dave?"

"You're speaking to the king, darlin'. Whatcha need?"

"Well, I was in your establishment earlier this morning, around five-thirty, and when I got home, I realized I had lost an earring. It's a blue feather. You wouldn't have happened to find it?" I held my breath, hoping on one hand that he said he'd still been closed at that time, which would incriminate Lacey, and on the other, wishing her alibi worked out and she was innocent, because really, who wants someone to be a murderer?

"There was only one woman in here today, real early this morning. Fake blond hair, fancy black nails, and the audacity to tell me to learn how to cook! That wouldn't have been you, would it?"

Sputtering for a moment against the insult about the hair color while Misty and Mabel moved to the living room to start a tug-of-war over the bag of chips, I finally said, "I mean, your skills could use a little help."

"I didn't find no earring," Dave growled in my ear, "but if I had, I'd have tossed in the trash. You ever darken my doors again, I'll throw you out on your rear!" He slammed the receiver down, and I winced, pulling my cell phone away from my ear. Once I could hear out of it again, I gave the girls a thumbs up.

"Her alibi checked out," I told them. I recounted what Dave had said, filling them in on everything I'd learned from Lacey. I also gave them an account of what had happened at Jesse's before pausing to pop an Advil, my head starting to hurt again.

We'd just started to cross out Lacey's name and move to our next suspect, who just so happened to be Jaime, when someone knocked on my door. It was Brey. At first, I thought something was wrong, because her cheeks were flushed, her dark blue eyes were bright, and she looked like she was about to pee on herself, but one word into her squeal and I knew the nineteen-year-old was just starstruck.

"Oh my gosh, Aubrey, there are two YouTubers downstairs! They want to talk to you."

I resisted the urge to roll my eyes as I followed her down the wooden steps, Misty and Mabel digging in my cupboards in search of more chips. YouTubers. They were like demigod celebrities, but their fanbase was way crazier than those of movie stars. And besides that, I have a checkered history with YouTubers. We have a fair amount of them come to Flamingo Springs and vlog their trip, and they give some of the businesses a boost, but while I like most of them, I've butted heads with a few. Namely with a popular beauty guru who'd insulted how I applied makeup, demanded free cupcakes, and shot footage in my bakery without asking permission. She was one of the rudest people I'd ever met and wore enough foundation to drown a bull.

After I'd kicked her out, she'd found a kindred soul in Vicki. The end result had been them doing a video together and trashing the bakery across the street without naming it. Obviously, it was mine, and it wasn't hard to find that out. For months, I received hate mail from the YouTubers' fans and lost a lot of business from the false reviews they put on my Google and Facebook pages.

It wasn't until after my lawyer got involved that the guru issued an apology video and retracted everything she said, turning on the tears for her several million fans. It'd only been a few months since that had happened, and last week, we had some weird dare-devil YouTuber come through. I've met other beauty gurus who were the sweetest souls in the world, but just like with cupcakes, it's usually the bad ones that leave the taste behind.

The social media stars flocked to my small town in droves in the summer, as we were a hotspot for Hollywood's biggest stars, thanks to Meaghan's Spa, which sat just outside city limits. It offered an array of treatments, and celebrities would retreat into one of the luxurious cabins for months at a time. YouTubers knew that one of the best ways to get views was either by featuring a movie star in a video, or touring Meaghan's Spa. They wasted no time in acquainting themselves with storeowners, as many were close friends with superstars, myself included.

Brey was doing a happy dance at the back door, excitedly beckoning to me as I stood there, feeling a bit woozy from my headache. I met her eyes, forcing a smile, and said, "Let's do this."

6

"What's up, beautiful people?" two male voices shouted, and I heard Terri let out a shriek of laughter, saying, "Do the voice. C'mon, do it!"

This was followed by a weird voice and phrase that made absolutely no sense to me, but clearly, it did to Terri, because she laughed again. Moving past Brey as she held the door open, I was greeted with the sight of my fifty-plus part-time help losing her mind over the two young men who stood in my kitchen.

She caught sight of me, her words coming out between gasps. "Oh, Aubrey, this is Mitch and Kasey, the YouTubers."

Studying the two men, both of whom couldn't be much younger than myself, I wondered if at some point in the last three days I'd gone through a wardrobe and just didn't know it. Both were clean and dressed in jeans and T-shirts that said California, and they wore sneakers, something that immediately made me warm up to them. There's just something about a guy who wears moccasins or those loafers that turn me off, so seeing sneakers was a good sign of how much I'd like these two.

Both had dark hair, one brown, one black, which they wore

short on the sides and long on the top. The shorter YouTuber had clear blue eyes that were only a shade darker than mine, while the taller one had brown ones, and both were holding a Dragon's Breath cupcake in their hands. I noticed neither held a camera and the frown that had crept up on me relaxed.

I studied them a moment longer. "I'm Aubrey. What can I do for you?"

"I'm Mitch," the taller one said, offering me his hand, "and this is Kasey. We own a YouTube channel and were wondering if it would be okay to film a bit of your shop." He gave me a friendly grin while his counterpart winked at Brey, who let out a nervous giggle. "We'll blur out faces if you'd like and follow any and every rule you give us."

Mitch gave my hand a firm shake and bit into his cupcake, still staring into my eyes. I felt a twinge of attraction. I tamped it down as the bell on the front door chimed. "Terri, Brey, I think someone's out front." I nodded at the YouTubers. "Why don't you guys go grab some folding chairs from behind that door," I pointed to the closet by the pantry, "and the card table."

Terri and Brey dragged their feet but finally left to help the woman who had come in and sounded like she wanted to buy most of the bread rolls. After setting up the table and chairs, Mitch and Kasey sat, looking at me expectantly. They were seated next to each other, and after shaking Kasey's hand, I sat across from them and said, "Why don't you tell me a little bit about your content, your audience, what your message is. How did you get started making videos?"

The next hour was spent listening to their history as Brey and Terri moved around us. As I'd suspected, they weren't that much younger than me. Kasey's twenty-fifth birthday was in two months, while Mitch had turned twenty-six the week before. Both had degrees in business and videography, and Kasey was currently enrolled in acting school. They took their YouTube channel seriously, and admitted that it probably wouldn't last forever, which was why they were both learning new skills so that when the day came, they would be able to find another occupation.

Texting Mabel and Misty that I wouldn't be coming back up, we agreed to work on our suspect list later. In between bites of a cupcake, Mitch described the message he and his best friend hoped to shout into the world, and they showed me numerous videos to help get their point across. Finding myself liking them, I agreed to allow them to film in my diner, and not only that, I agreed to let myself be filmed.

Mitch was the more vocal of the two, and he looked at me as he and Kasey folded the table back up. "We were thinking that we could do a cupcake eating challenge. You know, something fun that will make people laugh, but will also showcase your store."

"I don't think that would be a problem. It'd have to be after hours on Thursday, but I don't think Brey would mind baking. Is fifty enough? That'd be one of each flavor."

Kasey ran a hand through his dark brown hair, his green eyes wide. "We knew you offered a lot of flavors, but fifty?" He whistled. "I think I'm in heaven!"

The internet star's words made me laugh, then wince, as I reached up to rub my head. Seeing the concerned glance the two internet stars shared led into explaining what had happened, and since I couldn't just tell them part of the story, we ended sitting on the floor in the corner. Brey and Terri did their best to work around us, preparing plate after plate of food, tending to the steady stream of customers who found their way into the diner.

"Dude," Mitch said after I'd finished, "that's insane! Didn't the sheriff assign someone to protect you? I mean, it sounds to me like whoever this person is, they're messed up. Who finishes baking the bread of the person they just tried to kill?"

"Blaze thinks it's strange," I admitted, rubbing my forehead, "but what can he do? He and Stetson are the only two people on the force, and they can't spend all their time watching me. What if the killer goes after someone else?"

Kasey gave me a frown. "Well, we'll be around a lot, and since we're vlogging most of this trip, maybe we'll catch something on film."

Echoing him, Mitch stood, then gave me a fist bump. "If you want to see the footage before we upload, just text one of us."

"And let us know if you need us to stand guard," Kasey added.

Thanking them, I had a sudden thought. "Do you have a place to stay? The hotel fills up pretty fast this time of year, because a lot of people come for the Fourth of July party out at Cody's."

They assured me they did, having already checked in at the small hotel down the street, and after posing for a picture with Brey, they started for the door. "We're actually heading out to the Spa." Mitch's blue eyes crinkled at the corners as he smiled, trying to soften his rejection of Brey's offer of dinner. "We've got a session this evening and the plan is to film it. When we're traveling like this, we try to upload the same day we shoot, so once we get back, we'll probably hole up in our room and edit. Thanks, though."

Brey did her best to not look crestfallen as she sliced strawberries for a pancake platter. The diner was packed, and unless my two new friends left soon, it would only be a matter of minutes before Terri either told everyone in the dining area who was in the kitchen, or they were spotted.

I said as much and went past them to open the back door. Mitch went out first, mumbling something about wishing he'd parked out back instead of on the street, but Kasey hung back, obviously feeling a bit bad at having to turn Brey down. Though she was clearly a fan, she wasn't a crazy one, and I could tell he liked her.

Going over to where she was spraying a mound of home-made whipped cream on top of a tower of pumpkin waffles, he said, "Hey, you wanna be in our video Thursday? We usually have a lot of fun filming them."

There was no need to stick around to know what my wait-ress's answer would be. Once I made it back into my flat, I made a beeline for the bottle of painkillers in the bathroom cupboard. My head felt like it was about to cave in on itself, and after I swallowed the bitter white tablets, I stared at myself in the mirror. The soft yellow lights above the vanity couldn't hide the circles under my eyes, and despite my tan, I looked pale. I needed a nap, but from the sound of things, business was booming downstairs, and headache or not, my place was in the kitchen.

Splashing cold tap water on my face, I was blotting my cheeks dry when I heard a roar go up outside on the street. Exiting the bathroom, I went into my small living room and peered out the window. A black Humvee sat parked on the street a few stores down, and I could barely make out Mitch and Kasey as they struggled to autograph the several dozen napkins being thrust at them by the large crowd that had appeared seemingly out of thin air.

Chuckling, I watched them pose for selfie after selfie with their fans, and even though it was obvious they had somewhere to be, they lingered, clearly valuing their fans. Ranging in age from a young girl with eighteen bracelets on one arm, to a middle-aged couple who shook their hands, beaming from ear to ear, it was clear they reached a wide audience. Even after talking with them, I'd still felt a bit unsure about having them film in the diner, but now, watching them interact with their fans, I knew there was no way I could have said no and still have employees.

Feeling my phone vibrating in my pocket, I looked away

from the window, and seeing it was Mabel, I accepted the call, moving toward the door.

"You, me, Misty. Tonight, at Jesse's apartment. Wear black."

"I'm confused," I said, standing with one hand on the doorknob. "Why are we meeting there?"

Mabel let out a huff. "He's going to Houston to see his mom, and he won't be back until tomorrow. He just put the sign up on the store window. He's closing early and opening late. I think he's grieving, poor man."

"Okay." I drew the word out. "I don't get it. If Jesse isn't going to be in town, why are we meeting at his place?"

"Because," Mabel said, speaking very slowly as if I were hearing impaired, "he's on our list, remember? What better way to find out if he did Vicki in than to go through his apartment?"

Looking through the glass pane centered in my door, my pulse quickened as Blaze appeared at the foot of the stairs. "Are you insane?" I hissed into my phone as I jerked my hand away from the doorknob and made a beeline for the kitchen, fervently praying Blaze couldn't hear anything through the door he was now knocking on. "You want to break into Jesse's home and snoop?"

Mabel let out a breathy sigh that crackled over the line into my ear. "Unless you want to rot in a jail cell for something you didn't do, if the killer doesn't finish you off first, then yes, that's exactly what I'm saying."

Blaze thumped on the door again, and this time it wasn't the friendly tap it'd been the first time. This time, it was a sharp rap, like he was using his knuckles, and it sounded exactly like what it was. The knock of a cop.

"Blaze is here," I whispered into the phone. "I gotta go." I could hear the panic in my voice, my underarms growing damp with cold sweat.

"Either you meet me at Jesse's, or I come to your place and drag you there," Mabel snarled into my ear, and since Blaze was still waiting, I agreed, though it was most certainly against my better judgement. "Don't act suspicious," she coached me before hanging up. "I don't want to have to post bail."

"Really, Aubrey?" Blaze called through my door. "I know you're in there."

Tossing my phone onto the table, I took a deep breath before walking over and opening the door. "Blaze!" I exclaimed. I almost said, "I didn't hear you out there," but there was no way I couldn't have, so I knew that would sound suspicious. Then again, whipping open the door, practically shouting his name, then following it up with awkward silence wasn't any better.

Blaze squinted at me. "Your head feel okay?" he finally asked, scuffing the sole of one boot on the threshold, and realizing he was waiting to be invited in, I stood to the side and let him enter.

"It hurts," I told him, my eyes skimming over his broad back, admiring his defined shoulders, "but not like earlier."

"I see," he murmured, propping his hands on his hips and scanning my small flat.

"Um, excuse me?" I darted around in front of him as he stared at my living area, which was a bit messy from Mabel and Misty, who had left a chip bag on the couch and a stack of magazines scattered across the floor. "Can I help you?"

"Hmm?" Blaze said, looking down at me. "Oh, right. Just making sure you've got a secure place." He flashed me a megawatt smile. "Habit."

"Uh-huh," I stared at him. "I don't want to be rude, but unless you need something, I have to get down to the diner. They're swamped." A steady roar worked its way through my floorboards, along with Terri's loud laugh, and I was itching to get in the kitchen and start slinging pancake batter and bread dough.

Blaze started to answer but was cut off when my phone

started buzzing, and it was then I saw what I had tossed it on when I'd went to open the door. The list. Blaze saw it the same time I did, but I moved quicker, grabbing my phone up with one hand and silencing it—it was Misty—and stuffing the piece of paper into my pocket with the other before turning around.

"What was that?" Blaze asked me, taking a step toward the table, green eyes curious, but I only gave him a winsome smile.

"Nothing!" I chirped, taking a step back and around the table.

"You almost fell on your face to hide a list of 'nothing'?" Blaze quirked an eyebrow, his face cast into shadows by his hat, highlighting his lean cheeks. "What are you hiding, Aubrey?"

I pretended to look over his shoulder at the clock on the wall in the kitchen. "Would you look at the time," I said, "I gotta get downstairs!"

Whirling away, I moved for the door, all the while telling myself to be cool, act calm, and pretend that everything was normal. Blaze said nothing, following me out the door. He stood on the steps below me as I locked the handle, and I could feel his gaze between my shoulders. Because of everything that was going on, I inserted my key into the bolt lock and turned it, but by then, my nerves were shot, and my fingers were too sweaty to grip the key. I let out a growl after my third attempt to extract it.

When a tan clad arm snaked past me, I almost jumped out of my skin, resisting the urge to plaster myself against the side rail when Blaze's chest brushed my back as he worked the key loose from the twisted position I'd jammed it into.

"You know," he breathed into my ear, his breath warm on my neck, "despite what you think, I'm not the Big Bad Wolf."

Swallowing hard, I was suddenly very aware of how attractive and single he was, my skin so hot I thought it was going to catch on fire. A car rumbled down the street, the sound muffled by the building between us and it, and when I finally spoke, my voice was stronger than I thought it'd be. "Doesn't matter if you are or aren't, because last time I read the story, Little Red Riding Hood carried around a big ax and had herself some wolf stew."

I turned, my actions putting me nose to nose with Blaze, even though he stood a step below me. Plucking the keys from his hand, my fingers brushing his calloused ones, I gave him a confident smile, then squeezed past him and sashayed my way down the stairs. I was a bit overzealous though, because when I reached the landing, I tripped and stumbled in a graceless fashion. As Blaze let out a chortle from somewhere above me, I dove through the back door of my diner into safety, knowing he wouldn't follow me.

The next few hours found me scurrying around the kitchen, frying up bacon, kneading bread, slicing fruit, and getting a head start on the cupcakes for Brey. My headache finally subsided to the point I was willing to think about food, and once most of the patrons were happily chowing down on fresh, handmade goodies, I allowed myself a small break to eat. Terri loaded the dishwasher while Brey washed pots and pans, the oven timer set for twenty minutes as a seventh batch of cupcakes baked.

Pulling out my phone, I sent a quick text to Misty, asking her if she wanted to hang out, careful to not let on that I had anything other than dinner planned. If things went south, Blaze might confiscate my phone, and it would look pretty incriminating to have a text about breaking into Jesse's on there. She responded less than five minutes later, agreeing to come over, and, after finishing my water, I started frying bacon again.

Brey was still floating on Cloud Nine and wandered in to fix a plate of cupcake samplers for a table. Terri wasn't far behind her, humming under her breath. Apparently, they were still feeling the effects of Mitch and Kasey. Letting out a chuckle, all I could do was shake my head.

The diner stays open until seven or so on Tuesdays, and by the time I finished wiping everything down and mopped the floors, having sent Terri and Brey home at six, I was beat. It was past nine, and the sun was almost gone, the town cast into dusky shadows. Every little noise had me whirling around, ready to defend myself with whatever I happened to be holding. One time it was a broom, the next time it was a saltshaker, and I let out a sigh of relief when Misty knocked on the front door, clad completely in black, a dark beanie pulled down over her bright hair. Clearly, she must have met up with Mabel at some point and was ready to do some breaking and entering.

She helped me set out rolls of silverware for the next morning and waited in the kitchen while I darted upstairs to change, donning black jeans, a long-sleeved black shirt, and the darkest sneakers I owned, which turned out to be green. Since my hair is already black, I didn't need a hat. After pressing an ice pack to my head for a few minutes, I rejoined Misty.

"What's going on?" she asked as I ushered her out the back door, making sure to lock it. "Mabel told me to wear black and turn my phone on silent."

We made our way down the alley, coming to a stop right before it met the boardwalk. The sun had completely set, and a few stars were making an appearance. Peering around the corner, I looked down the street toward the police department, pleased to see it was dark. Neither Blaze's nor Stetson's trucks were anywhere to be seen.

"We're going to Jesse's," I hissed, taking one last look down the street before stepping onto the sidewalk. "Mabel thinks he might be holding something back, what with the way he tried to pin Vicki's murder on Jaime. And since he's gone tonight in Houston, we're gonna look through some of his stuff."

"You mean break in and snoop?" Misty whispered, grabbing my arm and yanking me to a stop. We were in front of Esposito's, and I peered through the floor to ceiling window, praying

Vincent and Maria had already gone home and weren't still cleaning up, because even I knew how suspicious we looked.

"More like furthering the arm of justice," I told Misty. "Besides, don't you want to find out who's behind everything?" I started walking again, dragging her with, since she was still clinging to my arm. We pressed ourselves against the front of buildings when we went under a light post, careful not to scuff our feet.

"You know I do," she muttered angrily. "But that doesn't mean I want to become a criminal to do it! What if we get caught?"

"We won't," I assured her, checking around us before stepping into a streetlight. "Now, come one, I wanna get this done and over with before breakfast."

Grumbling under her breath, Misty followed as I jogged across the street and into the alley between Jesse's store and Jeff's clinic. The shadow of the church across the street loomed over us, and I shoved a twinge of guilt away over what the good Lord was probably thinking about my law-breaking ways. I *had* to find out who was behind Vicki's murder, and if the only way to accomplish that was by breaking and entering, so be it.

It wasn't until Misty and I had slipped around the back of Jesse's building that it dawned on me that we didn't have a key, and no lock in Flamingo Springs was so outdated that the old credit card trick would work. So, unless Mabel had a key, it looked like we'd be literally 'breaking and entering.'

"There she is," Misty whispered, pointing, and I saw a small shadow standing by the stairs that led to Jesse's private quarters, jumping up and down, waving her arms like she was motioning a 747 in for a landing.

"We should have a signal," I breathed when we reached her, and though Mabel laughed, I was only half joking.

"Probably should leave that one in the movies," she whispered, "but good idea." She headed toward the stairs, every inch of her covered in black, including her hands, and she passed matching gloves to Misty and me. It wasn't until we were all crowded onto the small landing by Jesse's door that I got a good look at her face in the dim light that shone through the glass pane from the lamp that had been left on.

"Are you wearing face paint?" I asked, doing my best to keep my voice low, but even Misty must have thought Mabel was a little over the top, because she started laughing. She held onto the guardrail as she struggled to keep quiet so that we didn't wake up Mike and Jack, who lived in the apartment next door above an empty store.

"Well, duh," Mabel responded, shoving a key at me. "You think I wanna get caught?"

Fumbling the key, I almost dropped it, since it was a bit hard to hold onto with the gloves I'd donned. When I finally got it into the doorknob, I looked down at her as she pressed against my side, my face slick with sweat. "Where did you get a key?"

She shushed me and almost shoved me through the door, pulling Misty with her, who'd just slipped on her own gloves, and it wasn't until she'd lowered the shade over the now closed door that she answered. "Way back, before you two lived here, I actually lived in this apartment. I never got around to giving the key to Jesse when he bought the empty store, and he apparently has never changed the lock." She winked at me, her round face dark with hunting paint. "If it hadn't worked, you'd be running back to your place for a hammer right about now."

At Misty's indignant gasp from across the large and sparsely decorated living room where she was already rifling through the drawers of a desk that was pressed against the wall, Mabel chuckled. "Relax, Misty, I was joking. You use a crowbar, not a hammer."

Looking past the arguing duo, I noticed I could see Mike's living room window through the one in Jesse's kitchen, and even as I realized what I was looking at, a light clicked on in the widower's home. "Get down!" I hissed, dropping to the floor, my elbow connecting hard with the wood flooring.

Misty obeyed, almost knocking herself out on the corner of the desk, but Mabel just froze, as if Mike would look right past her if she mimicked a statue. From my place on the floor, which, to my surprise, was almost as clean as my counter tops, I could see the top portion of Mike's window, and less than ten seconds after it came on, the light went out. We breathed a sigh of relief, Mabel quickly moving forward to shut the shades on all the windows, using drawers she opened as steps to climb onto the counters to do so.

Climbing to my feet, I groaned as my elbow started to throb, while Misty muttered something rude under her breath as she moved toward the bookcase. Mabel was going through the kitchen cabinets, and looking around as my friends skillfully snooped, I realized the only place left to look was the bedroom.

In the two years I'd known Jesse, I always thought he was a super clean guy. You have to be when you run a grocery mart, and his flat was no different. The wood flooring actually squeaked under my sneakers, and there was the distinct smell of cleaning products in the air. Even in the near darkness I could tell that not a book was out of place, and as I slowly made my way to the bedroom, running my fingertips along the walls to keep from bumping into them, I could hear Mabel rummaging through the kitchen, exclaiming over this and that.

Jesse's bedroom was bigger than my living room, and after making sure the shades were shut, I pulled my phone out of my pocket and turned the flashlight app on. Holding it out in front of myself, I did a slow circle. Apart from the small dresser that stood against the far wall and a floor lamp by the left side of the bed, Jesse's room was empty, with only a few pictures on the walls that I presumed to be of him and his mother, since the tall blond bore a strong resemblance to him. I leaned closer to one picture and realized that Jesse kept a tight mouth about himself.

He was in Marine dress blues in a few and fatigues in one, and now I understood his strong sense of cleanliness and scarcity of personal items. I looked toward the dresser, my stomach queasy. It just didn't feel right to go through his stuff. How could I treat a veteran with such disrespect? Not that I felt all that great about doing it even before I knew his past.

I shook my head. Veteran or not, I had to find out who killed Vicki. I eased open the top drawer of the dresser. Eight pairs of neatly folded socks greeted me. Running my finger along the wood beneath them, I found none of the dust that normally accumulates there. The second one was the same, containing shirts that had been folded into perfect squares, a stack of boxer underwear next to them. The third and final drawer was filled with more shirts and a pair of worn slippers, and I even tapped different areas of the dresser to see if there was a false bottom anywhere.

The closet was the same. Sweatshirts and pants were spaced along the metal rod on hangers, almost as if Jesse held up a ruler to make sure the distances were exact. A small shoe rack held two pairs of sneakers, a pair of dress shoes, and, of course, a pair of cowboy boots that matched the hat that sat on the shelf above the clothing rod. Unlike most closets, Jesse's was void of clutter of any kind, and when I looked under the bed, there was nothing but a clean floor.

I'm a neat person myself, but when you have tile or wood flooring throughout your entire home and you live in a desert, there's bound to be some dust. Not so for Jesse. His floor was so shiny I'd be willing sleep on it. When I rejoined Mabel and Misty in the kitchen where they were searching every last cupboard, I found they had run into the same problem.

"The man owns only the basics," Mabel said, obviously frustrated as she shut the doors to the garbage can that sat beneath the sink. "And everything is stacked exactly so. Do you know how hard it is to investigate when you have to make sure you're putting everything back just as it was?"

"Tell me about it," Misty sighed putting up a hand in front of her face when I accidentally shined my flashlight into it. "His bathroom is so pristine it makes me wonder if he's ever even used it."

"Three years I lived here," Mabel sniffed, finally accepting defeat and turning her light off, "and even if I cleaned every day, I could never have gotten it to look so tidy."

I looked around us, at how empty the apartment seemed, how colorless everything was. The living room was a reflection of the bedroom, and all in all, it just seemed like a poor excuse for a home.

"Lonely," I said out loud, startling myself, and when my companions looked at me, I said, turning off my light, "it's lonely here. I've never thought about it before, but I don't think Jesse has many friends."

"You're right," Misty agreed. "That must be awful, coming home to this every night."

It was on the tip of my tongue to mention the pictures in the bedroom but something stopped me, and I motioned for the door after checking my phone. "We need to go. Mabel, you should probably open the shades again so that he doesn't suspect anything." I lifted a foot. "As it is, seeing how orderly he is, we're going to be lucky if he doesn't figure out someone was in here just from the floor."

"I don't think he did it," Misty said, taking pity on Mabel and opening the shades, a dark ninja with strands of pink hair escaping her hat. "There's absolutely nothing here that points at Jesse being anything other than boring and clean." She opened the last shade and we headed for the door.

"Yeah," Mabel sighed. "And since I scouted out the store this afternoon, there's nowhere else to look. I think he's a dead end."

Echoing her sigh, I reached for the doorknob. "But we have plenty more people on that list who have bigger reason to kill Vicki than Jesse. Like Cody."

"All I know," Misty whispered as we locked the door and slunk down the stairs, "is that I'm really glad church is tomorrow night, because I need to do some serious repenting for what we just did."

Mabel chuckled even as I agreed with Misty. "Honey, start saying your prayers now, because what we did tonight is nothing compared to what we're doing tomorrow."

7

W ednesday found me back in the kitchen, serving up plates of hot food and cold milk, and after I'd seated Mitch and Kasey, I scurried back to the kitchen for the coffee pot.

"Haven't seen you guys for a while," I said to Vincent and Marie Esposito as I filled their coffee cups. Brey wasn't scheduled to show up until noon, so I was burning some serious sneaker rubber as I trekked back and forth between the dining area and kitchen.

Marie gave me a smile, the corners of her black eyes crinkling up as she stirred creamer into her cup. "We've been swamped lately," she said. "Every night, it takes all we have. We might have to start requiring reservations on the weekends."

Vincent nodded as he looked over the menu, seeming to be stuck between pancakes or the hash brown bowl. "Yes, but we realized we've been so busy working, we haven't been able to spend time with our friends."

Marie opted for the muffin platter. He ordered pancakes, then added, "And since everyone appears to be dying off, we thought we'd better go around and say goodbye to everyone, since we don't know who might be next."

Eyebrows attempting to take flight, I self-consciously brushed the tender spot on my head hidden with a colorful bandana I'd wrapped over it and knotted into my bun. "That's kind of a creepy thing to say." Suspicion colored my tone as I eyed him.

He shrugged. "But it's true. We don't know who might be next. It could be us!"

Marie swatted his arm. "Really, Vincent? A woman gets murdered, and that's your plan? Start saying goodbye to people?"

"I'm going to go get your meal cooking," I said, taking a step back. "Let me know if you need anything else." I made a hasty retreat to the kitchen and took a deep breath as I prepared their plates. Vincent's strange words chilled me to the bone, and I wondered if he was warning me. Though, if he was the murderer, that wouldn't make sense.

My fridge hummed loudly over the quiet murmur of conversation from the dining area as I leaned against it. Only two days had passed since Vicki's death, and already, every single person I thought I trusted suddenly looked like killers. I didn't like it. Instead of bringing the townspeople together, this tragedy was pulling us apart. It made it hard to serve people, and I didn't know how I would ever be able to look Jesse in the eye again after what I'd done last night.

Going back out, I placed Marie's muffin platter in front of her and Vincent's order by his arm, along with a jar of maple syrup. Marie was bent over her phone, scrolling through what looked to be Facebook. Setting it aside, she looked up at me. "You heard that there's not going to be a funeral tomorrow, right?"

"Uh, no." Pulling a roll of silverware from my apron pocket I handed it to the young couple a table over because their toddler had just thrown his on the floor. "Why not?"

"It's been changed to a memorial service instead," Marie answered. "Her actual funeral is Friday, in Houston, for immediate family only. So, Pastor is putting on a slideshow and asking people to speak."

"I can't imagine losing someone like that," I murmured, moving away to seat a large family that was ambling in. Mitch and Kasey were already gone, though they had left me a nice tip. Looking out the large bay windows that made up most of the front of my shop, I saw them making their way toward the hotel, Mitch holding a camera in front of them while Kasey gestured wildly.

"No," Vincent shook his head as I came back by. "And only the good Lord knows what's going to happen now."

Not sure if he'd been given a different medication for his ulcer issue and it was messing with his brain, or if he was giving me subtle warnings, I took a cautious step back. Either way, I had no interest in sticking around to find out. I had too much to do, and since Blaze had just come in, looking rather disgruntled, my list had increased.

Motioning him back to the kitchen, I started more coffee and threw some fluffy pancake batter on the griddle. I'd recently added a new item to the menu that seemed to be a favorite among those with kids, and it was one of my favorite guilty pleasure snacks—hot fudge stuffed pancakes, topped with a rich peanut butter drizzle. Blaze took his position against the counter across the kitchen and watched me create my newest masterpiece. After a few seconds, I started feeling a little uncomfortable.

I already had a guilty conscience from what I'd done the night before, though Mabel had showed no remorse when she'd texted me earlier. Misty had simply told me to drop it, and I was sure that I had a neon sign on the back of my shirt that flashed 'I did it!' Not exactly what you want to be feeling when the sheriff is trying to stare a hole into your brain.

After the silence extended to the awkward stage, Blaze spoke, and I flinched, the ladle of batter I held poised to drizzle on the griddle jerking up and over my shoulder. The words, "Jesse's apartment was broken into last night," were punctuated with the sound of gooey batter slapping the floor and splattering the shirt of a cowboy who was probably ready to strangle me.

Still holding the ladle, I whirled. "No!" I gasped. "Is nothing safe anymore?"

Blaze ran a finger through the white batter sliding down his uniform and brought it to his lips. "Not bad," he said, his dark green eyes meeting mine and holding them. "Sweeter than most."

The words, 'like you,' hung in the air between us before they fell to the floor, just like the substance dripping from the ladle I was holding, and he pointed at it. "You should probably put that down."

Obeying, I wiped my mess up from the floor, and once he'd cleaned his shirt, he again pinned me with those keen eyes. "You wouldn't happen to have any idea of who could have done that, do you, Aubrey?"

As a Christian, I believe that honesty is the *only* policy. I also believe that breaking the law is sin, unless the law is telling me to go against God's word, because He does command us to obey the law of the land. I'd went against the beautiful truth of the Bible enough times in the last two days to last me a year, and when I opened my mouth, looking Blaze right in the eye, I knew I couldn't tell a lie.

"I do," I said slowly, heading past him to place the glass container of homemade peanut butter sauce in the microwave. I hit the thirty second button and looked up at him, the arms he'd crossed over his damp chest mere inches from me as I stiff-ened my back.

Blaze quirked an eyebrow, pausing before speaking to let the burst of laughter from the dining area die down. "Wanna expound on that a little more?" He shifted his left foot forward, the tip of his boot brushing against my blue sneaker, the badge he wore shining into my eyes with a righteous gleam.

"I want to," I told him, "but I'm not going to." I moved away from him to grab the peanut butter sauce from the microwave that had dinged and went back across the kitchen to finish preparing the pancakes. "Unless that means you can arrest me."

Drizzling the sauce over the thousand-calorie meal, I looked at him over my shoulder. "You wouldn't arrest me though, would you?"

This time it was Blaze who crossed the kitchen, and when he spoke, his voice had lost all semblance of teasing. "I have the right to if I believe you're withholding information that could further my case. And since you just admitted you know who did the breaking and entering, but are refusing to elaborate, and since this is most likely connected to the murder investiga-tion, a lawyer would have a tough time getting you out."

The sound of the doorbell tinkling as someone entered barely registering in my ears as they pounded with blood. My mouth went dry. Blaze stepped nearer and leaned down so close I could see the flecks of black in his clear eyes and smell Old Spice. "However, since I'm pretty sure this is nothing more than busy-body women trying to solve an investigation that's best left to the professionals, I'm willing to let it go."

It was my turn to quirk an eyebrow as I set the container of peanut butter sauce on the counter. "Why do I feel that there's a 'but' coming?"

He grinned, a dangerous look on such a good-looking man,

and said, "Because there is. I'll make you a deal, Aubrey, and you're going to take it, because I don't have to and probably shouldn't be offering you one. I'm going to pretend that this conversation never happened, and you're going to mind your own business and keep your rear in your diner making cupcakes."

"Mind my own business when a killer is running around knocking people out and probably stalking his next target as we speak?" I snorted, grabbing up the plate and pushing past him to stalk toward the dining area. "I think not."

Storming out to the young family's table, I gave them the giant platter of stuffed pancakes and a refill of coffee. Once I'd checked on the rest of my customers, I headed back to the kitchen, only to be waylaid by a hand on my wrist. Before I could protest, Blaze had me pinned against the wall by the phone where no one could see or hear us from the dining area or the kitchen, his lips pressed into a thin line, and a shiver raced through me.

"Snooping around will only get you hurt," he hissed into my face, "while staying home could very well be what saves you."

"Really?" I scoffed the words at him, working very hard to not be affected by how close he was to me. "Wasn't that what I was doing when I got beaned upside the head?"

"Aubrey," Blaze ground out, "this isn't some stupid little game. People are getting hurt and I can't keep an eye on you all the time. I won't say it again. Stay out of this."

His head had tilted lower and lower with each word, until the brim of his hat brushed my forehead and his nose was almost pressing against mine. "If I didn't know better, Sheriff," I quipped falling back on humor since all intelligent thought had fled my brain the moment he'd grabbed me, "I'd say you actually care about me." I said the words with a sweet smile and a tap to his chest with the hand that wasn't held in a tight grip.

Thinking he'd respond with something equally flirty since that was quickly becoming something we did, I was surprised when, if possible, he turned even more serious. "Maybe that's why I'm telling you to stay out of this," he rasped. He shook his head, his hat brim moving back and forth across my face. "But clearly, unless I lock you and your friends up, which would mean no more cupcakes, you're going to keep snooping."

He stepped back, releasing me as the doorbell tinkled again. "Use your head and stay safe, Aubrey. If you're gonna be a snoop, be a smart one, and don't take any chances. I don't want to have to add your file to the shelf Vicki's is on."

He turned. "Have a good day." He strode across the kitchen toward the back entry, and it finally sunk in how worried he was. Right before he twisted the doorknob, I called his name. He froze but didn't turn around.

"Will it help if I tell you anything I find out?"

Broad shoulders lifting in a heavy sigh, he only nodded before opening the door and disappearing into the bright sunlight that poured down from a cloudless sky. I spent the rest of the morning pondering his warnings as I served customer after customer, wondering if I should obey him and leave the investigation up to him.

By the time Brey showed up, I'd almost talked myself into it, too, until I was bussing a table and looked out the window and across the street at Vicki's empty shop. My stomach clenched painfully. Gritting my teeth, I determined that Blaze or no Blaze, I wouldn't give up until Vicki had justice, no matter what I had to do.

Terri showed up around two, though she carried a department cell phone on her hip should an emergency call come in and shooed me out of the kitchen. "It's been barely a day since you got your head split open," she scolded me while Brey sighed over a text message that I assumed was from Kasey. "Go hang out with Misty or something, but I don't want to see you anywhere near here for the rest of the day."

Giving her a smart salute, I snapped my heels together.

Who was I to argue at a day off? Besides, at the moment, the diner was completely void of customers, so what harm could it do to leave for the rest of the day?

"Yes, ma'am!" Before Brey could start gushing, I was gone, beating a path to Misty's. I went out the front door instead of the back, and since I was too busy looking over my shoulder admiring how good my store looked to pay attention to what was in front of me, I walked straight into a wall of flesh, and a good smelling one at that.

"Whoa there!" Strong hands grabbed my shoulders and steadied me as I started to fall backward. Looking up, I found myself staring straight in Cody Jackson's dark blue eyes. Though the dude ranch owner had darkened my diner's doors at least once a week since I'd opened, I still wasn't sure if I liked him. Cody was the type of guy women of all ages swoon over. But, unlike other cowboys, say, for lack of a better example, Blaze, he wasn't someone a girl took home to her mama.

Cody was tall, with thick blond hair he wore in a stylish cut and eyes the color of ripe blueberries. He had abs of steel from spending his time on the backs of bulls, and his triceps had triceps. He was a shrewd businessman who was also a playboy, running a successful ranch while still maintaining a top spot in the world of bull riding. I'd lost count of how many belts he'd won, how many reporters had swarmed my shop asking where the hunk lived, but no matter how attractive he was or how charming he could be, I'd never been able to warm up to the smoldering cowboy, and he knew it.

Part of that, I think, was because even when I'd first moved to Flamingo Springs, he and Vicki had sorta been a thing, and my distaste for her had bled over into my feelings for him. Now, he stood inches away from me, a slight grin teasing the corners of his mouth, tanned cheeks ready to bring forth the dimple I think all cowboys are born with.

"I'm gonna start calling you 'Burning Rubber Aubrey,'" he

teased, drawing the words out in a sweet southern drawl that had provoked more than one woman to blush. "Always runnin' somewhere."

Despite his teasing words, I could sense the sadness that hung about him like it was hanging around everyone in town, and mustering up my best smile, I said, "How 'bout a free cupcake as an apology?" I tried to step back, aware that he still held me by the shoulders.

After a pause, he released me, letting his tan arms fall to his sides. "I think it sounds like a pretty sweet package." He winked. "Just like you."

Even though Cody had no shortage of female admirers, he never let that stop him from flirting with almost every woman he met. Misty loved it when he came around, though it was becoming no secret that she had a thing for Stetson. And, I have to admit, my pulse sped up just a bit every time I saw him.

Stepping back inside, we turned after hearing Mabel's voice. Barreling around the high glass counter that housed sweets, she gave him a piece of her mind. Apparently, hitting on me only days after his ex was murdered was a no-no in her book, though, in Cody's defense, I think flirting with every woman he saw was just part of his charm.

"Cody Jackson!" she cried indignantly, shaking her short finger up at his nose, "You should be ashamed of yourself, carrying on in such a way after what happened!"

Mabel can be quite dramatic. Even though she painted Cody as a suspect only the day before, she'd also been the person he'd confided in, so I wasn't surprised when her outburst was met with a bemused expression.

"How am I carrying on?" he asked in a confused tone, blue eyes darkening. I only shook my head when he glanced my way, raising my palms in the air. Brey and Terri had gone suspiciously quiet in the kitchen, and I knew they were probably

KERI LYNN

90

pressed against the wall by the door, ears craning to catch every word.

"Weaseling a cupcake out of Aubrey the day after you got one out of me!" Mabel's fierce expression switched from angry to playful, and the shaking finger was now a wagging one. I was just as confused as Cody. All of that show for a cupcake? It wasn't until she sent me a wink that I caught on that this was about more than the sweet treat, and luckily, Cody was too busy apologizing to notice her signal.

Giving a little chuckle, I left the two arguing in the diner about how many times was too many to beg free dessert out of me and headed for Misty's. Terri and Brey were finishing up baking for the video with Mitch and Kasey, and since Suzanne had called that morning asking me to supply the sweets for Vicki's memorial service, they'd be starting on those before long.

I'd chosen a simple coffee and caramel cupcake, two of Vicki's favorite flavors, having read about it in her obituary. Because they were for her, I'd instructed Brey to add pink dye to the batter, since pink was the primary color Vicki's shop was decorated in, and once they'd set, I would carefully infuse them with a mixture of coffee liqueur and caramel, almost like you would to a poke cake. It was an original recipe, one I'd never make again, but it'd go down in my recipe book, once I got it back, as Vicki's Cupcakes.

Taking my time getting to Misty's, I stopped to admire storefronts as owners put up Independence Day decorations. Filling their windows with red, white, and blue crepe hangings, stars were plastered all over glass doors, and the 'We Support Our Troops' posters were front and center.

My shop was in the middle of town, sandwiched between an empty one-story barn and Dirk's law office, though he was rarely in town. The side of Flamingo Springs that held the Sheriff's Office, Jesse's, Jeff's office, the church, and a few other must-have businesses was referred to as the business section. Starting at the hotel and going down to the other end, which included my shop, Lacey's, Esposito's, Vicki's, Misty's, a few tourist shops, two jewelry stores, a boutique that served fancy lemonade, and two clothing stores, was known as the downtown.

This was the side of town I loved to be on, and as I strolled down the plank sidewalk, I waved to the storeowners as they fixed up their windows. Most of us were either single, or married with no children, so when the town was void of tourists, like it currently was, it was quiet out. That silence wouldn't last long though, because the Fourth of July was only a few days away. At the minimum, a hundred people would fill the hotel that sat at the end of the street by Misty's and overflow out to the spa and Cody's ranch for the bash he threw every year.

I waved at Mike as he and Jack walked down the opposite side of the street. Being a single dad, Mike was also home-schooling the little fellow, and clearly, it was time for a field trip. They'd be at Cody's ranch, too, because who would want to miss the roasting of an entire pig, all the watermelon, potato salad, root beer, and sweet tea they could eat and drink? Vincent and Maria always supplied a big spread of garlic bread and cold soups, and Jesse brought the ice cream, since he had a gourmet section of it at the Mart.

There were always dozens of games to participate in, horse-back riding, and watching the cowboys perform tricks. Once the sun set, we gathered together in Cody's spacious backyard and had a bonfire. Since my arrival in Flamingo Springs, the Fourth quickly became my favorite holiday, even surpassing Christmas.

Busy dreaming about the succulent slice of pork I would have, it took me a minute to figure out I was standing in front of Misty's glass door, staring into space while my mouth filled with drool. It was at this time I also noticed I was blocking about a dozen women from leaving. Stepping to the side, I gave them a sheepish grin and a mumbled apology as I held the door open.

They trooped past me, and once they'd disappeared down the street to the parking lot behind the boutique, I went inside. The first thing that struck me was how cool it was compared to the dry heat outside that sucked every bit of moisture out of your skin, and the second thing that hit me was the giggles coming from the back studio. High pitched and definitely belonging to Misty, they floated across the air, accompanied by the low chuckle of a man. I hurried across the room, worried her kombucha had gone rank and left her a bit tipsy.

Skidding into the small studio she reserved for smaller classes, I came to an abrupt halt at the sight of my normally cool and reserved yoga friend batting her eyelashes up at Mitch while twirling her cotton-candy pink hair around one finger. Kasey stood several feet away, securing a camera on a tripod, having already set up ring lights. He was turned away from me, and since the other two were a bit busy flirting with each other, it wasn't until after I'd nosily cleared my throat and reentered the room that they saw me.

"Aubrey!" Mitch greeted me, a grin splitting his handsome face as he finally tore himself away from Misty. "You're just in time to be our helper."

Giving him a blank look while Kasey moved behind me, muttering something about proper lighting even as Misty unrolled a yoga mat, I crossed my arms. "I beg your pardon? Helper? Do you see a tag on me anywhere that says that?"

Misty laughed. "Come off it, Aubrey! We're making a video. You can hold up flashcards for us."

"Making a video?" I muttered back like some sort of recording monkey.

"The Yoga Pose Challenge," Mitch said, kicking off his

sneakers and stacking them by a backpack that leaned against the lavender wall that was supposed to induce feelings of calmness. "It's a big hit all over the internet, and what better time to make a video of it than with an actual yoga instructor?"

I took his question to be rhetorical and focused on Misty as she started a few warm-up stretches. "You've got to be kidding. You hate being filmed, and now you're making a video?"

She shrugged. Mitch and Kasey left the room to change into yoga apparel. "Mitch said he could help me start a channel, and in my free time, I can upload videos of practices." She looked me straight in the eye as she did a lunge. "Think of the people I could reach with my message, Aubrey. Millions." She switched to downward dog. "And even it doesn't work out, it'll be a good hobby to take up." Misty smirked at me and straightened. "Besides, with a hunk like Mitch offering to help me learn the ropes, do you really think I'd say no?"

There didn't seem to be a reply to that one, and since Mitch and Kasey were filing back into the room clad in yoga attire, my brain couldn't come up with a good retort. I don't think anybody's can when they're trying not to combust from laughing. It's one thing to see Misty outfitted in her yoga pants and a snug tank top, but it's a whole other realm to see two full-grown men dressed in it. Kasey, with his lanky frame, looked like a plucked flamingo, his comically bright pink pants almost blinding, and the aqua blue long sleeve shirt he wore wasn't much better. He paraded in front of me and struck a diva pose, blue eyes gleaming, and I snorted even as Misty cheered.

When it was Mitch's turn, he strutted past me like he was walking to music, wiggling and shaking to a beat no one could hear but him. When he sent me a coy look over his shoulder, I cracked, laughing so hard my eyes watered. He'd forgone pink altogether and painted on a pair of purple pants. I realized the city boy was fitter than I'd thought, his black shirt leaving little to the imagination. While cowboy boots and Wranglers were more my style for men, I still let out an appreciative whistle, which won me a kiss that Mitch blew from across the room.

"Two things to know about filming," he told Misty as he and Kasey put bright yellow sweatbands around their foreheads. "Number one is that we don't expect perfection. The best videos are the ones that have mistakes. Our biggest goal with our channel besides spreading a positive message is spreading laughter, and people love to laugh at other's mistakes. Number two is probably the most important. Have fun."

Kasey nodded and broke in, saying, "If we're having fun, the audience is going to have fun. Don't focus on the camera, focus on what's going on." He snapped a sweatband over his wrist and flexed his thin arm. "Now let's get this party started."

He'd set up three cameras around the room to catch the skit at every angle, and while he turned them on and did last minute adjustments, Mitch gave me his phone and asked me to google difficult yoga poses involving at least two people. I would show them the picture, which would be edited to appear on the screen with the video, and Misty would try to walk them through performing the pose.

Before we began, she had me lock up the front, just in case someone wandered in. After a few false starts, they started filming. It was a bit awkward at first, and I could tell that my normally calm friend was tense with nerves, but as Mitch and Kasey went through the intro of the video and introduced her, I could see her loosening up a bit. What followed was probably the best forty-five minutes of my week. I laughed until I had to excuse myself to the bathroom watching them try to form the poses, because not only were the two internet stars terrible at yoga, they were hilarious about it, cracking jokes left and right. When it was done, they had the footage they needed. Mitch was sporting a large tear in his shirt, and Kasey nursed a bruised elbow, both having occurred when they'd tried a pyramid pose, lost balance, and hit the floor.

We gathered in the kitchen where we watched some of the video, downing some huge smoothies Misty made, Mitch insisting the recipe had to be included in the description of the video. When he was done praising my yogi friend for her smoothie skills, talk turned serious. Kasey brought up the subject we'd pushed as far from our minds as we could.

"Have you found anything out?" he asked, finishing his drink, and I shook my head. "I was in that grocery mart today and I heard the owner saying someone broke into his house last night. You think it was the same dude who killed your friend?"

Misty and I shared a long look before I rubbed the side of my still sore head as Mitch pecked at the laptop. "Well, no. I don't."

Mitch looked up, pinning me with a hard gaze, though it softened when he momentarily glanced at Misty. "You sound pretty sure of that." He lifted an eyebrow at me, brown eyes quizzical, and letting out a guilty sigh, I shook my head.

"I am, because I'm the one who did the breaking and entering." I gave Misty a sideways glace even as she stirred what was left of her smoothie with a wooden straw. "Well, we did. Us and another friend."

"Why?" Kasey asked, and though his question was only one word, one syllable, the lack of judgement in his tone made me cave, and I decided to let them in on what we had done.

"So, you found nothing but a guy who falls into the category of being a clean freak?" Mitch was pecking away at his laptop again, making a list of things that didn't add up about the case, and this time it was Misty who spoke.

"That's correct, yes. But we do know that whoever killed Vicki has to live around town, because the only way they would have gotten in her shop was if she let them, since Blaze said the back lock hadn't been tampered with. We thought of Jesse because they dated once or twice, but he has a solid alibi, as does Lacey."

"What about your sheriff, or his deputy?" Mitch asked. To his amusement, Misty and I spoke at the same time.

"Blaze?" I blurted out incredulously while Misty exclaimed angrily, "Stetson?"

We looked at each other. "No," I finally said. "No way in a million years could Blaze or Stetson be our murderer." The very thought of it made me shake my head.

"Just because they wear a badge doesn't mean they aren't capable of crime," Mitch said, but I crossed my arms over my chest.

"Stetson is probably the sweetest guy I know," I told him, giving him a bit of the evil eye while Misty echoed me. "And Blaze is too straight-laced and too by-the-book to even jay walk."

Mitch held up his hands while his quiet counterpart bit into an apple. "Okay, I guess that wasn't too bright of an idea to suggest the men who mean so much to you. But, what about the people who own that Italian place, or that Cody fellow? What about the boutique owners, or the woman who owns the spa? She seemed pretty chill when we were out there the other night, but that doesn't mean anything."

"Meaghan never leaves the spa," Misty said, "so she's an out, but as for everyone else, I have an idea. Today is Wednesday. We have church tonight, and since we just had a murder, I bet it's gonna be a full service. Why don't y'all tag along and take in everyone? Maybe you'll see something Aubrey and I can't because you aren't friends with everybody."

"Jaime should be there," I said, "and while Blaze has written her off, I haven't. I just can't forget how she acted when Jesse brought up the business influx she'd get since Vicki is gone." Seeing the confused looks on Kasey and Mitch's faces, I filled them in on the scene that had happened at Jesse's Mart the day before, and Mitch added another note to his laptop.

"She's looking like number one," he said, Kasey leaning over his shoulder, "and I think that Cody guy is number two. He's a man with everything, but she jilted him anyway, so that makes him look pretty suspect."

"What about a number three?" I asked, and Kasey took a loud bite of his apple before saying,

"I think Lacey, from the hair salon. I've read a lot of stories about how exes turn crazy, and even though she has an alibi, I don't think we should trust her all the way. She may not be an ex, but she seems to have some pretty strong feelings for Cody."

Mitch closed the laptop as Misty and I nodded. "I think coming to church tonight is a great idea, and besides that, even though you've said nothing about your pastor and his wife, they should still be looked into." He stood, checking the clock on his phone. "And while these are all probably trails the sheriff has already gone down, it can't hurt to follow them. We might see something he didn't, and sometimes people are more willing to talk to us than they are to people they know."

"Service starts at seven," I told the duo. "Don't be late. We've got great music." Bidding them farewell, I texted Mabel, wondering where she was and what her big plan for the day was since the bakery was closing in only a few minutes, but she didn't reply.

It wasn't until after Misty had showered and changed into jeans and a T-shirt that Mabel showed up to the studio, hauling a notebook with her. Pink shoes dusty, she wore a triumphant look on her face, as well as a smear of chocolate by the corner of her mouth.

"We've got a new suspect," she crowed, shoving past us to climb into a chair and look expectantly at Misty until she brought Mabel a glass of milk.

She downed half of it and let out a big sigh before wiping

her mouth and giving us a big grin. "We're not begging," I told her, tapping one toe on the floor as I glared down at her, and when Misty only nodded, Mabel rolled her eyes.

"You two are no fun," she muttered, but she opened the notebook, pointing at an entry she'd made. "But, since I'm such a nice person, I'll tell you what I found out anyway."

We sat down on either side of her, and she tapped the page. "Jeni, who owns that jewelry shop just down from Aubrey, told me that Vicki had started selling the same products she was, but for way cheaper prices. Turns out, Vicki was buying costume jewelry replicas and selling them as the real deal to the young female tourists who come through, and it was costing Jeni a lot of business because Vicki was selling them at a super cheap price. Jeni told me over a plate of cupcakes and some iced tea that she confronted Vicki about it and went to Blaze. But the only thing he could do was tell Vicki to put up a sign saying they were replicas, since she only ever 'alluded' that they were real."

"Jeni told you that today?" I asked doubtfully. "Doesn't she know that makes her a suspect?"

"She told me that six months ago," Mabel replied.

Misty nodded. "I vaguely remember hearing something about it," she said, "but I didn't realize it was to such a degree."

"Oh yeah," Mabel said. "And that's why I said we had a big night tonight, or whatever it is I told you last night, because she was around number four on my suspect list. But today sealed the deal for me. I went into the shop to look for some earrings for the memorial service to go with my dress, and I overheard Jeni on the phone. I don't think she knew I was in the store, because she didn't turn around, but what I overheard gives her a pretty good motive for murder."

Stomach burning, I realized how close we could be to finding out who had killed Vicki and end this nightmare once and for all, but I only choked out, "What'd you hear?"

Mabel leaned back in her chair her nails making a rustling noise over the sequined flamingos on her shirt as she scratched her shoulder. "She was on the phone with a financial advisor asking them if bankruptcy was her only choice. Jeni is facing financial ruin because in her words, 'That witch down the street stole my business with her fake stuff.'" Mabel looked at us with wide eyes. "You know what that means, guys? Jeni could be the killer. She's leaving town tonight to go to Houston, so I think we should sneak in and check out her apartment."

Goosebumps rose on my arms, and I looked at Misty. "That does give her a pretty good reason for murder, doesn't it?"

Misty gave me a funny look. "I don't feel good about this," she said. "This vibe feels really off."

"Because we're getting close," Mabel insisted. "It feels bad because Jeni is probably the one who did it."

"Yeah," I said, rubbing the back of my neck, "but Jesse knows someone was in his place last night. What if she does, too?"

"She won't be back for a week. After a week of being gone, no one remembers exactly what condition their house was in, especially if you drink like she does."

"Still," I paused. "This doesn't feel right."

Looking at Misty, I expected her to side with me, but instead, she took Mabel's side. "I think we should do it." She held up a hand at my protest. "Aubrey, I know how you feel about it, but if we don't find out who killed Vicki soon, they might strike again, and if this can prevent it, then perhaps we should do it."

Looking back at Mabel, I nodded. "It's settled then. After church, we're going back to being sinners."

8

C hurch was a blur for me that night. While I did register happiness at Mitch and Kasey being there, soaking in the simple but deep teachings of Pastor Brent after being led in worship by Suzanne, I honestly don't know what the lesson was about. Brent could have been teaching about alien conspiracies and Bill Gaither being an angel in disguise, and I wouldn't have noticed. Although Misty and Mabel, both seated to my left, didn't seem to be having the same problem, Blaze did, because every time I looked away from Brent as he made some point using the overhead, Blaze was staring at me, and it wasn't the admiring kind of stare. It was an 'I know you're up to something and I *will* find out' kind of stare. It sent shivers down my back—the bad kind,.

As Misty had predicted, church was packed. Everyone wanted to get their affairs in order with the Lord should their number be called by the killer. And since Mitch and Kasey were there, I was content to let them watch everybody and gather info. It'd been only two and a half days since Vicki had been killed, and I was already worn out from suspecting every-one. Besides that, my head was hurting again, and the small band-aid Misty had put over my wound before service was pulling at my hair.

Church was over by nine, and people began filing out to go home, though when Brent had ended the service at eight-thirty, there'd been such a flood of souls to the altar, I thought the Lord had spoken and I missed it. Mitch and Kasey were gone by the time I went outside with my friends onto the dusty street, and I could just make out their backs as they headed for the hotel, talking a mile a second into a camera.

Just like the night before, Mabel, Misty, and I changed into black clothing and waited for the town to fall asleep before heading out, passing the hours by eating cookies dunked in milk. We even got in two episodes of NCIS before it was time to go breaking and entering. Mabel declared she'd be Gibbs, leaving Misty and me to fight over who got to be Tony and who had to be McGee.

The only dark side to the fun evening was when I'd broached the subject of Mabel and I meeting one day soon to go over her recipes. It was a monthly tradition of ours, meeting for a few hours to share the recipes for new food concoctions we'd created and trade notes. A good deal of my best sellers were Mabel's creations. She was always giving me notepads filled with her neat handwriting, but instead of excitedly suggesting the next morning to meet like she always did, she sent me an annoyed look over the top of her coffee mug.

"I don't really have anything to share with you this go around," she practically bit out.

The sudden change in her demeanor caused Misty to put down her glass of celery juice and stare at her from the far end of the couch.

"I think I'd rather start keeping them to myself, if you don't mind," Mable added.

Struggling to keep my mouth from falling open as I floundered for a response, I sent Mabel a weak smile. "Sure. I mean, that's no problem. I just thought, you know, since we've been doing it for the last two years ... I didn't realize you didn't want to ... Um, yeah, that's no problem." I finished my stammering ramble on a high-pitched note, Mabel gave me a short nod before turning back to her phone, ignoring the TV in front of us.

The whole exchange was a bit weird and left me with a bad taste in my mouth. I blamed Mabel's unusually sour behavior on stress from the case and left it at that, but the conversation continued to bother me. It was always in the back of my mind, making me wonder what was coming over my friend to cause her to act so rudely. It was as if for a brief moment, a curtain had been pulled aside to reveal a deep anger in her eyes, and it was almost as if it was directed at me.

I bit my lip. If I wasn't careful, I was going to become paranoid, and then I'd be of no help to anyone. Mabel just wasn't feeling well. There was no use trying to get more of it than that. She was human, just like me, and to extend a little grace to her wouldn't kill me.

Forty-five minutes later, we skulked down the street, and since I was still balking at the whole idea of breaking into someone's home again, Mabel decided to leave me outside as a lookout, just in case someone came by who knew Jeni was out of town. "I'll open the kitchen window," she told me, pointing at the small window that faced the road. "If you see or hear someone, let out a bird call."

She stationed me across the street down a small alley between June's Boutique & Fashion and Ryan's Flamingo Springs Gifts and Tokens, one of the few alleys that didn't have a streetlight. Sound travels pretty far on a clear Texas night, and she and Misty would have no trouble hearing me from my position. Once they started off across the street, I settled back into the dark shadows of June's building and waited.

Flamingo Springs is a quiet place, even in peak vacation

season, and since all the stores are closed by nine at the very latest, tourists are in their hotel rooms by nine-thirty. Though I strained my eyeballs until I thought they'd pop out of my head and listened so hard my ears started ringing, there was no sign of life on the street.

Behind me, apparently, was a different story, because about fifteen minutes after Mabel and Misty disappeared across the street, a hand clamped down on my shoulder. A squawk left my mouth, and whirling, I found myself facing a tall man with a bronze star on his chest that glinted in the faint glow the street-light across the road cast onto it. My turkey imitation quickly turned into a groan.

"Nice evening to be out," Blaze greeted me, his hand now wrapped around my wrist. "Strange place to be spending it, but I try to not judge people for their life choices."

"Just out for a walk?" I suggested, but when he only shook his head, cowboy hat making a small breeze across my face, I knew I was doomed.

"You scared the blazes out of me," I hissed, jerking away from him, now angry at how I'd not only let myself be jumped, but also at how my stomach was dancing with butterflies.

Blaze let out a chuckle, my insult clearly not bothering him. "At least it wasn't something else." He took a step closer, his chest brushing mine as he stared down at me. He kept getting closer until I backed out into the street where I could fully see him in the streetlight, the dim stars above us not even making a dent on the darkness that surrounded us. "Not twelve hours after I tell you to be careful, I find you out in an alley while your friends break into yet another house."

"I don't know what you're talking about," I said indigently, but my angry words were lost as Blaze laughed once again before snaking an arm around my waist and jerking me against him.

"You're a horrible liar, Aubrey." His teeth gleamed in the

light, but when I looked into his eyes, their green depths glowing, I found no response in my throat, and for that matter, no breath either. He raised his voice so that it carried across the street. "When I'm done kissing you, Mabel had better not be digging through Jeni's fridge."

There was a yelp, then a crash as Mabel fell off something, and my ears filled with a roar. Blaze looked back at me, a grin stretching his lips. His eyes were the last thing I saw before my own closed. He lowered his head and laid a kiss on me that would shame a teenager. We're talking movie scene stuff here, and when his free arm wrapped around my upper back, crushing me against his chest, my arms moved against my will, moving up so that one was flung around his neck. Fingers reaching up, I knocked the hat that often hid his thick hair to the ground, my other hand resting on a broad shoulder before I pressed it against his chest.

Though I knew I should pull away, I couldn't find the will to do so, and when Blaze increased the temperature of the kiss so that we were outdoing a Ghost Pepper on the heat index scale, I knew I was fighting a losing battle. It was like all the annoyance I'd felt at him since he'd become sheriff, all the sparks of attraction, the frustrated anger I'd harbored against him, came out to combust into a kiss so hot, a kiss so wild, I felt like I was about to shoot up into the sky like a bottle rocket. The walls I'd spent years building around my heart came crashing down, jolting me with the realization that Blaze was nothing like my ex-fiancé.

When he finally pulled away, I followed, jerking his head back down to mine, his chuckle tickling my lips as it rumbled through his chest and into mine. A chorus of coyotes had started up somewhere out on the grassy plains beyond our dusty town, and for just a moment, I realized that all those romance novels just might be right. Perhaps my knight in shining armor was actually a country boy in a cowboy hat. The slight stubble on said country boy's chin rasped against my jaw as he ended the toe-curling, firework-igniting kiss.

It was only then that I remembered we were standing in the middle of the road illuminated by the streetlight, and if anyone looked out their window, they'd see us, two adults who usually avoided each other, locked in a rather passionate embrace. The thought finally moved me away from Blaze, though I immediately missed the warmth of his arms. From the toothy grin he gave me, I don't think he had the same inhibitions.

"I always thought kissin' you would be like eatin' one of those Dragon's Breath cupcakes," he said, resting one hand on the butt of his gun, the other propped on his opposite hip, "and boy, was I right. Sweet and spicy, the best combination ever invented."

The rebuke that had been forming on my lips died as his words sunk in. He bent to pick up his hat, dusting it off before plopping it back on his head. *Blaze had thought about kissing me?* Face flushing so hot I probably looked like a neon sign, I swallowed my words, realizing I'd just stepped over a line that could never be crossed back over. I'd just kissed the enemy.

Okay, so maybe Blaze wasn't exactly my enemy, but for the last ten months, he'd been nothing but a man who irritated and sometimes flirted with me. In the short span of three days, he'd suddenly become something much different, and I wasn't sure if I liked it or not.

He jerked his chin in the direction behind me. "Looks like they cleared out." He turned, starting down the street toward my building. "It's getting late. I'll walk you back."

Finally ungluing my tongue from the roof of my mouth, I hurried to catch up with him after taking a glance at Jeni's window. It was shut. There was no sign of life in her apartment or her store, and I could only assume Mabel and Misty were waiting for me back at my place. I resisted the urge to groan, knowing I'd never hear the end of what had just happened.

Catching up to Blaze, I spoke. "You usually leave town around eight. Why are you still here?"

Sending me what I guessed to be an amused look before answering, his boots made almost no noise as they puffed through the dusty street. "You do your homework." He chuckled. "After everything that's been going down, Stetson and I figured it'd be best if one of us stayed the night at the office, just in case something happened. He'll be on tomorrow night."

Turning down the alley by my store, we stopped by the stairs that led up to my apartment. "We're actually more concerned about keeping an eye on you and the two M's than we are with anything else. And since we weren't wrong, I guess he owes me lunch tomorrow."

I could hear the faint rumble of my TV as Misty and Mabel laughed above us, clearly unconcerned about where I was, but before I could go join them, I knew I needed to level with Blaze. After sitting down on the second to bottom step, I patted the empty space next me, and once he'd sat down, I spoke.

"I wouldn't do it. I couldn't break into Jeni's house after how I felt about going into Jesse's. It's wrong. We have to find out who's behind everything, but tonight felt off."

"So, you were made lookout," Blaze interjected, and I nodded, leaning forward to rest my arms on my knees even as he leaned backed and propped his elbows on the step behind him.

Telling him Mabel's theory about Jeni, I breathed in the slight scent of his aftershave. It was as if we were just two friends having a late-night conversation and enjoying life, not discussing theories about who might have murdered Vicki. In the darkness that surrounded us, I could almost forget I was one of Blaze's top suspects, and when the crickets started chirping, it was all I could do to not lean against his shoulder.

"It's a good theory," he mused once I'd finished my explanation, staring out into the darkness of the plains that surrounded our small town, "and it's not one I'd looked into." He sighed. "But something about it doesn't sound right. Yeah, Jeni lost business because of what Vicki did, but I don't think it was near enough to cause her to file bankruptcy."

"I know," I answered quietly. "We're missing something."

Blaze rose, a smooth motion that belied the hours he spent working at his ranch, and following suit, though in a much less graceful manner, I stood next to him, resting one foot on the bottom step.

"I've been a cop for a long time," he finally told me, "and I've seen a lot of crazy stuff. If there's one thing I learned, it's to always trust my gut. The mind will conjure up all sorts of stuff that ain't true, and the heart has a habit of following emotions instead of facts, but the gut ... My gut has never been wrong, and right now, it's telling me we're chasing after the wrong bull."

Facing me, his badge once again caught the light. "There are some things I can turn a blind eye to, Aubrey. For other things, I'm willing to ignore them a few times, but that's it." He stepped closer, his dark gaze searching mine in the faint light of the moon that was beginning to rise. "Get what I'm saying?"

"Stay inside after dark?" I asked weakly, knowing that the next time he caught me breaking and entering, I wouldn't be rewarded with a kiss.

Grinning, his white teeth flashed in the light. "Spot on, sweetheart. Spot on."

9

"One more word," I ground out at Terri the next day as we set up for Mitch and Kasey's video, "and you'll be out a paycheck." I slammed a stack of paper plates onto the folding table that was set up in the bakery kitchen, giving her a foul look. The two YouTubers would be arriving any minute to start filming, and since Brey was in the bathroom touching up her makeup, Terri and I were left to get everything ready.

Like most of the other businesses in town, I was closed from noon to four in observation for Vicki's memorial service. Glancing over at the container that held the dessert I'd named after her, a twinge of sadness went through me, though it was quickly pushed away by Terri's smirk as she placed a tray of cupcakes on the table. She was decked out in a dark blue sheath, and the curly brown hair streaked with gray that she usually wore in a strict knot was pulled away from her square face by pins. It was one of the few times I'd seen my friend in something other than a uniform or jeans, and she looked beautiful. I said as much.

"Thanks," she replied. She eyed me as I stood back to

survey the kitchen, taking my apron off. "So do you." She snickered. "Blaze will probably think so, too."

The glare I leveled at her was weak, as it's hard to look fierce
when you're blushing. I looked down at my outfit, a simple
sixties-style black dress with black flats. I'd twisted my hair
back into a bun and had applied some concealer to the
sunburn on my nose. I shook my head. I don't know why I was
worried about what Blaze would think. It was a memorial
service for crying out loud! And on top of that, it was for
someone who'd been murdered.

And besides, as I'd adamantly told Misty and Mabel last
night after I'd left Blaze at the bottom of the steps, I had no
interest in the handsome sheriff. None whatsoever. I was
attracted to him, there was no denying that, but I was in no
danger of falling for him.

Mabel had accused me of fearing being left at the altar
again, though Misty had remained quiet on that one. She'd
simply gazed at me with her wise eyes before slipping away to
her apartment. I knew that at some point, she'd bring up the
subject of being open to love again, something she touched on
with me every so often. If I truly trusted God, I wouldn't be
afraid to open my heart.

Shaking my head, I scowled at Terri. "I don't care what he
thinks. Today is about Vicki."

She nodded, taking off her own apron. "You're right. I'll wait
until tomorrow to start this up again." She turned as Mitch and
Kasey came through the back door even as Brey finally
emerged from the employee bathroom. Kasey almost dropped
his armload of tripods as he gaped at her, and I have to say,
even I was a bit taken back at my waitress's appearance.

Brey was a beautiful girl, almost twenty years old. She'd gone
with a pair of ripped jeans and black bullrider's tank top, and,
staying true to her country roots, had kept her broken-in boots.

Long blond hair pulled up into a messy look, she'd added a touch of mascara and lipstick. Glancing back at Kasey, who was still standing in the middle of the kitchen while Mitch carried in a second load of supplies, it was clear he was smitten with her. Finally setting the tripods down, he let out a nervous cough. "Wow. You look really nice, Brey."

My waitress gave him a flirty wink and sashayed her way over to him, the smell of Chanel No. 5, the perfume all women use when they've set their cap for a man, filling the room. "Thanks," she practically purred.

Meeting Mitch's gaze after he rolled his eyes, I snickered, though we both meant it good-naturedly. "We're heading out," I informed him, since Kasey looked like he was a few planets away, and Brey was too occupied flirting with him while making it look like she couldn't hear me. "I'm not sure when we'll be back, hopefully around three, so take as long as you need. Drinks are on me, so whatever you find in the fridge, have all you want."

I started to turn away to follow Terri through the dining area, then whirled back, grabbing the container of cupcakes. "Also, I left some bacon in the fridge in case y'all didn't get breakfast."

Leaving the kitchen, I was almost to the front door when Mitch caught up with me, grabbing my arm and pulling me back. "We think we found something that can help you guys out," he said, hazel eyes dark but appreciative as he let his gaze wander the length of me as I set the cupcakes on a table.

Propping a hand on my hip, I was in no mood to be flirted with. I had two different reasons for that, one being that I was going to a memorial service, the other being, well ... "And that would be?" I asked, looking up at him as he scuffed a sneaker on the floor.

He bit his lip and looked away, releasing my arm to tug on

the hem of his tee shirt. "Could be nothing," he said, "might be something, but we thought you should see it."

He looked up. "That Cody guy was snooping around your shop last night, right after you closed. You must have already left, because he knocked on the door a few times, and when no one answered, he tried to get in. He looked steamed, too. We only saw it when we were editing our vlog last night, and once he saw us, he took off."

We didn't even know he was in town until we went to our room last night and heard a bunch of noise outside. His truck was parked in that back lot, and he was standing next to it while he and that blond chick from the salon yelled at each other. I think he thought she was here."

Mitch shrugged. "He left after about ten minutes of it, and so did she, but when we talked to you yesterday, you said that those two weren't on speaking terms because he's a player, and she's sick of it."

"If they'd lie about something like that, they could be lying about their involvement with Vicki's murder," I said slowly, and he nodded, clearly upset.

Reaching out, I touched his tense forearm, his hands now jammed into his pockets as he glared at the floor. "You're on vacation right now, Mitch. Don't worry about this."

He shook his head, a faint grin touching his lips as Kasey and Brey laughed in the kitchen, having started the party without him. "To be honest, Aubrey, Kase and I have been feeling a bit at odds with everyone lately." He looked up, and I removed my hand, not wanting to send the wrong message. "Don't get me wrong, I love Los Angeles, and I would never dream of living anywhere else, but it just seems like other people in our profession are getting shallow. Kase and I try to put out the best content we possibly can, and it's hard to watch your friends succumb to putting out cheap videos and turn from being normal people to being petty. We've lost a lot of friends this past year because we won't stand for a lot of the drama that's been going down, most of which is fake. We love our fans, and watching other creators use their fanbase only to make money and not a community has been putting a wedge between a lot of us."

He lifted a shoulder in a sigh. "Coming here was like coming home. I know we only met like, two days ago, but I consider you to be a friend." He cocked his head and sent me a wink. "I even like your sheriff. And friends are there for each other. We'll help you find the killer, Aubrey, no matter what happens."

For a moment, I could only stare at the young man before me, very aware of the fact that he was offering friendship, something that was hard to come by. Before I could answer, he pulled me into an embrace. "You're always welcome here," I finally whispered into his ear as I hugged him back, feeling like I'd just met a brother I didn't know I had. "Our home is yours, and I think it'd be awesome if you and Misty got together."

Mitch pulled back, eyes suspiciously bright. "Thanks," he said huskily. "That means more to me than you'll ever know. Except for Kasey, I've never actually had family, just kinda bounced around from place to place once I got out of the orphanage." Looking over my shoulder, he laughed and said, "But you had better repeat what you just said about me and Misty to your boyfriend, because he looks like he's about to strangle me."

Before I could correct Mitch about my relationship with the Blaze, he was gone, and I turned to see Blaze glaring at me through the front door, Mitch's chipper voice joining in with the other two in the kitchen. I couldn't bring myself to look Blaze in the eye, settling my gaze on the floor. Only when he stood in front of me, having opened the door and walked in, did I look up at him.

As usual, he was dressed in his sheriff's uniform, and the

only nod to the service we were about to attend was the black bolo tie around his neck. His boots were shined to perfection, and with his utility belt riding snug around his hips and black hat clamped on his head, he looked like he'd just posed for an Inspirational Romance book cover shoot. Except this was real life, and last time I checked, I was still a murder suspect.

"Thought I'd escort you over," he said, eyes skimming my dress, lingering on my cheek. He reached out and thumbed a spot on it. "Flour," he explained when I raised an eyebrow. After grabbing the cupcakes, I exited the diner through the door he held open, wishing with all my might that I could crawl into bed and hide under the covers until this nightmare was over.

Once on the sidewalk, Blaze offered me his arm and I didn't hesitate to take him up on his offer. What had happened last night would be dealt with a different day. As we walked toward the church, I saw that most of the shops had done the same thing I'd done, temporarily covering the bright Fourth of July decorations with black crepe.

Arriving at the church, I left my cupcakes on a table in the fellowship hall and made my way into the sanctuary, Blaze finally releasing my arm to talk to Jesse, who was dressed in a dark gray suit. Stetson, also wearing his uniform, talked in low tones to Lacey, whose eyes were bloodshot as she worried a Kleenex to shreds. I think up until that moment, it hadn't truly sunk in for me exactly what had happened. Sure, I knew Vicki was gone, I knew I'd never see her again, but somehow, it hadn't hit home until I entered the church and saw pictures of her everywhere, placed between the flowers Pastor Brent and Suzanne had ordered. Vicki was dead, and her killer was roaming free.

Finding a spot by Misty, Mabel seated a few rows back and to the left, I sat down, trembling. Vicki was gone. The woman I'd loved to aggravate, who'd been nothing but a thorn in my side, but who also watched out for me, was gone. When Brent started speaking, reading some scripture and sharing his favorite memory of Vicki, Misty started crying, the black net she wore over her pink hair bobbing as she struggled to hold it together.

"We know of Jesus' promise in Matthew," Brent said. "To take heart, for He has overcome the world. Jesus has overcome death and the grave, and while her life here is over, Vicki's life with the Lord has only just begun. I can imagine that she's already baking for him and the Apostle Paul, and has probably decorated her mansion with pink cowboy décor."

The audience chuckled at that one, though my laugh was wet. After Suzanne sang "I Can Only Imagine," Brent opened the platform to anyone who would like to remember Vicki. Looking around, I saw that no one had any intention of doing so. Slipping out of my pew, I made my way to the platform, where a surprised Brent handed me the mic.

Looking out over the congregation, I took a deep breath. "I think my favorite memory of Vicki is when she told Paul he couldn't eat at her diner unless he shaved his mountain man beard, and if he did, the meal would be on the house." I laughed. "And he did, because no one in their right mind would pass up a chance to eat Vicki's incredible creations." I spied Cody in the second to front row, his black suit sung over his shoulders, his tie looking like it was about to choke him. "And I remember when she told Cody Jackson that he had one more time to track mud into her diner, and she was gonna pin his hide to the wall."

Looking out at everyone, I searched for Blaze, and when I saw him, leaning against the back wall, I gazed into his eyes, begging for strength. When he nodded, I went on, surprised to find myself struggling to speak past the rock in my throat. "But what I remember most about Vicki was how much she loved to give. A lot of y'all probably don't know this, but every Saturday, after she closed, Vicki would drive to Houston with all the left-over baked goods and visit old folks. She had a big heart, and even though I know she's up in heaven probably trying to tell God how to run everything, and I know she's feeling nothing but joy, she's left a pretty big hole down here."

Eyes filling with tears, I drew in a shaky breath. "I'm not much of a singer, but I know this was her favorite song, so if you don't mind, I'd like to share it with you." I started singing the opening lines to "When I Get Where I'm Going," a song that had rocked the country world with its release, one that I'd heard playing in Vicki's shop more than once.

Halfway through the chorus, tears were streaming down my face, and I had to force myself to keep singing as one by one, the audience joined in. I looked out across the mourners, seeing the grief on each face, but it was Mabel who caught and held my attention as I finished singing. Like everyone else, she was crying, but unlike them, she wasn't just shedding a few tears, she was weeping, and it struck me as a bit odd. Yes, Mabel probably cared more for Vicki than most of us, but her loud sobs surprised me, and I almost lost my place in the song.

Letting the last note trail off, I handed the microphone back to Brent before making my way toward the back of the church. Full as it was, with more people coming in while I'd sang, there was no way I could get back to my seat without disrupting the service, so I decided to join Blaze at his spot against the wall.

He gave me a long look, chewing on his lower lip, green eyes shadowed with an emotion I couldn't put a name to, but after a moment, he pulled me against his chest and wrapped his arms around me in a tight embrace. I leaned into him, gathering strength from him, aware more than ever of how much danger I could be in. When I finally pulled back, Brent's words of encouragement and hope surrounding us, I saw that almost everyone was hugging. Jesse was holding Misty, Mabel was crushed against Tom's chest, and even Cody was showing emotion as Jeff quietly talked to him. I realized that Vicki's death was weighing on us all.

At Brent's dismissal, we trooped into the fellowship hall where a spread of food was laid out on some folding tables. I helped myself to a slice of watermelon, my stomach rebelling against the thought of anything more than that, and looking around, I saw that I wasn't the only one. Many of the towns-people didn't even bother to grab a plate, sitting in huddles around the tables that were decorated with green and pink tablecloths.

Blaze, however, had no such inhibitions, and snagging a plate from the stack by my elbow, he proceeded to load it with a sample of every dish laid out. After setting it on a table, he headed back to grab a glass of lemonade. Clearly, funerals didn't disrupt the sheriff's digestion system like it did ours, but, then again, from what I'd heard, Blaze had been a cop for a long time in a rough city and was probably a bit desensitized to the whole thing.

Turning away, I looked for my friends, but when I saw they were seated next to Jesse and Cody, I decided I'd rather sit else-where. I still couldn't look Jesse in the eye, and I knew he had to suspect something after the awkward way I'd treated him that morning when he came in for a donut. As for Cody ... Well, the cards were still out about him, and since the Fourth was coming up in only a few days, he was the next person on my list to be investigated.

Independence Day was Sunday, and I only had three days to prepare for the event. From Thursday morning on, I would be up around four and wouldn't get to bed until midnight, because the Fourth was the day I sat in a booth out at Cody's ranch. He charged thirty dollars a head for an all-you-can-eat buffet that lasted the entire day, and while half of my creations would be donated, the other half would bring me a sight of money. That meant I would be too busy baking to do anything else. So, until Sunday arrived, the investigation was on hold.

Looking back toward Blaze, seated at a table by himself, hat next to his plate, shoveling food into his mouth like he hadn't eaten for a week, I moved forward before I could talk myself out of it.

"How can you eat right now?" popped out of my mouth as I sat down next to him, placing my paper plate with its tiny helping of fruit in front of myself.

He paused before taking another bite of potato salad that was neon yellow with mustard. "'Cuz I'm hungry," he said after swallowing, and once he'd taken a good swig of the lemonade, he bit into the baked chicken leg.

Taking a small bite of the watermelon, my jaw clenched at the sweetness that flooded my mouth. Looking around, I realized that Blaze had chosen a spot that allowed him to watch everyone and everything. Peeking at him from the corner of my eye, I saw that while he was still munching away on the chicken, his eyes were moving, taking in everything that was happening. I tried to look at the people in front of us like a cop would, seeing them not as friends or people I knew, but as potential suspects, my mind trying to figure out who was capable of murder, but I couldn't. No matter who I looked at, I had a reason as to why they couldn't have killed Vicki. Just like with investigating Lacey, Jesse, and Jeni, I saw no motive strong enough to make them want to kill.

My gaze landed on Cody and stilled. Even though he was next on the list Mabel had written, I struggled to see him as anything but a fun-loving, hard-working, sometimes snobby cowboy.

Blaze let out a grunt, and I looked back at him. He'd scraped his plate clean and emptied his glass and was about to stare a hole through Cody's blond head. Clearly, the sheriff didn't have the hesitations about the dude rancher that I did, because his green eyes were narrowed, lips thin.

The quiet rumble of voices almost covered my whisper as I leaned closer to Blaze. "You think it was him?" This close to him I was strongly aware of the scent of aftershave that rose from his tanned neck, and the slight stubble on his jaw caught the light, showing hints of red and gold.

He turned his head, green eyes boring into mine, and despite myself, I felt a blush burn its way up my neck, and my sleeveless dress suddenly felt too tight and too heavy. I could almost hear the shocked whispers of those around us as they watched me have what looked to be an intimate conversation with a person who, up until three days ago, I'd had no problem wrinkling my nose at.

Blaze's eyes crinkled at the corners as he smiled, one hand reaching up to smooth back his hair, which he wore long enough to style but short enough that he didn't have to if he didn't want to. "Nope," he said quietly, still staring at me. "Pretty positive it wasn't him."

Turning my attention back to the person of interest, I rolled my eyes as he flirted with Misty, Lacey scowling at them from a table away. Vincent and Marie were slipping out the door, waving goodbye as they called it a day, and Brent loosened the tie around his throat as Meaghan, who had graced us with her presence instead of staying holed up at her spa, spoke to Jeni.

"Then why do you keep looking at him like that?" I shifted back to look at Blaze.

One hand flat on the table, the other resting on the butt of his gun, he glanced at me, then back at the crowd. "Let's just say Cody and I have the same interest in something, and I'm not about to let him have it."

The tone he used when speaking was conversational enough, but one look at Blaze's jaw let me know that he'd fight Cody for whatever it was they were interested in. What that something was bemused me, because I could think of nothing that they would have in common. Seeing the expression on my face, Blaze laughed.

"It's not hitting home, is it?" he asked. When I shook my head, he let out another laugh. Leaning close, he tugged on my chin until I faced him, my satiny skirt rustling against the rough material of his pants. "Should I explain it?" he whispered in a husky voice, and while I was deciding whether or not to nod, he looked back over at Cody, who was now staring at us one eyebrow raised even as a slight sneer touched his lips.

The two men held eye contact as Blaze brushed his lips against my cheek before getting to his feet. The smirk Cody sent me had me seeing red, and I shoved my chair back. Hard. It screeched across the floor and the room fell silent, everyone staring at me. Grabbing my plate of watermelon, I stalked to the garbage can and threw it in. The only sound in the room was that of my skirts rustling as I stomped toward the door, which I yanked open.

Used to female drama, though usually from Vicki, not me, everyone started talking again before I was even all the way over the threshold. I was almost across the street, my flats making puffs of dust in the bright sunshine, before my arm was grabbed and I was jerked to a halt.

Without even looking I knew the calloused fingers wrapped around my wrist belonged to Blaze, and I glared down the street toward my shop. I wanted nothing more than to go start a batch of bread, the dough providing me with something to pound my emotions out on.

"Really, Aubrey? Really?" Blaze had the nerve to sound annoyed.

I whirled, jabbing the pointer finger of my free hand into his chest. "Don't 'really' me, Blaze Martin," I bit the words out, earrings brushing against my cheeks as they swung with my motions. And *emotions.* "Of all the gall and nerve, I can't believe you just did that!"

Blaze had the audacity to looked confused, but the twinkle in his eyes gave him away. "Did what?" he asked innocently, letting me go and raising both hands in the air, chest flexing under my finger.

Glaring at him, I was ready to breathe fire. Or paw the ground. Burn him or run him down, either one sounded good to me at the moment.

"I am not some dog or piece of property to be fought over, and if you ever do that again, I'll smack you so hard you'll think your mama just caught you smoking a cigar." I stamped my foot with the last word, meaning every bit of it, because for the first time in a long time, I was angry.

Despite what modern fiction says, being fought over by two men is everything but exciting. It's infuriating, embarrassing, and demeaning. If two men are vying for your heart, that's a different story, but to be fought over as if I was nothing more than an acre of land? To have someone stake their claim on you as if you're nothing more than an innate object? And the kicker of it all was I knew Cody had no interest in me besides harmless flirting. It ticked me off that not only was he knowingly leading Blaze on by pretending to like me, Blaze was taking the bait, and I wondered aloud if he was this stupid in the professional world as well.

The grin that had been toying at the corners of Blaze's mouth dropped, and he scowled, a look that any other day would have had me trembling in fear, but only served as fuel for the fire today. "Is that a threat, Aubrey?" he asked softly, referencing my earlier comment of slapping him. I snorted, letting my hand drop to my side, thankful, even in my frustrated state, that everyone was inside and wasn't witnessing the showdown.

"Yes, Mr. Officer, it is," I said. "And you can take it to the bank and cash it." I started walking toward my diner. "Shall I explain that to you, Sheriff, or do you think you can figure it out on your own?" I tossed him a glare over my shoulder as he stared after me. "Make sure you go and look in your little law book to make sure you can't write me a ticket for sassin' you, cuz I'm sure you're just itching to whip that notepad out!"

I stepped up on the plank sidewalk and stormed to my diner. As I yanked the door open, I saw in its reflection that he was still standing where I'd left him, and sweeping over the threshold, I lifted my nose. Come Sunday, Cody Jackson was going to get an earful and possibly a cupcake to the face for his part in this. But even as I stormed through the dining area, I couldn't help but wonder if he was trying to distract Blaze into seeing him as a jerk and nothing more, throwing any suspicion of murder off him.

The emotions from the night before were gone, leaving me clearheaded and back to square one with the sheriff, which was just how I liked it. He stayed on his turf, I stayed on mine, and that was that. I was still going to do my best to figure out what was going on in Flamingo Springs, but the ideas of sharing my theories and suspicions with Blaze were gone, as were my dreams of kissing him again.

As far as I was concerned, Blaze was the sheriff, and nothing more.

10

"Mitch and Kasey uploaded the video last night, and it's already gotten over a million views." Brey's hyper voice filled my ears as we loaded my jeep with crates of goodies. The early morning sun was already hot as it bore down on us, and I was thankful for the light breeze that had come up.

Having parked my Jeep outside the front of my diner the night before, we now filled it, and all around us, other shop owners mirrored our actions. From eight to noon, vendors were allowed to operate at Cody's ranch. After that, the food would be set out. From there on, it was a day of pure relaxation and fun.

Though it was supposed to be the day of my date with Darren, he'd called the night before with the news that neither he nor his brothers would be attending the celebration. A close member of the family had passed away, and surprisingly enough, I was relieved. After almost two years of wishing he'd ask me out, I'd been ecstatic when he'd approached me Tuesday. Now, I wasn't so sure about my feelings for him and was grateful for some extra time to figure them out.

It was currently a quarter to seven, and I looked up at the sky, pressing my hands against the small of my back. My shirt damp with sweat, I saw a film of haze forming above us, a sure sign of a scorching day. Not that I minded. A hot Fourth of July meant thirsty tourists, and from the looks of the several dozen who were milling around the streets, the lemonade and iced tea I would be offering wouldn't be a problem to sell.

The thought of cold drinks brought a frown to my face, and Brey laughed as she pushed past me to load another box. "C'mon, Aubrey, it's Independence Day. Turn that frown upside down! Today's gonna be beautiful!"

Though normally a cheerful person myself, I felt like strangling my waitress, and she held up her hands, backing away as she laughed. "Or frown. Whatever you want."

She darted back into the diner, and I sighed. Brey couldn't help being so happy, it was just part of her nature, and now that she and Kasey were quickly becoming an item, she was even happier. She'd clearly found a guy worth giving a second look, and if the soupy grin on Kasey's face was any evidence as he and Mitch strolled toward us, he thought the same thing.

As usual, Mitch held a camera in front of them as they documented their vacation for their fans, and seeing Stetson make his way down the street, they approached him, asking for a quick interview about what to expect for the Fourth. He obliged, tilting his hat back. I knew, despite the fact his back was turned to me, that he was flashing his megawatt grin at the camera, and his hazel eyes were probably crinkled just a tiny bit at the corners as he spoke.

The deputy had shared a late dinner with me the night before, both of us up until almost one as we waited to hear from Terri that she'd made it to her daughter's house a few towns over. I'd worked on finishing everything up for my booth at Cody's while Stetson had run over everything with the new part-time assistant deputy Blaze had hired two days previous, a wet-behind-the-ears kid who was eager to serve his community. He was a young nineteen-year-old who wanted nothing more than to become a hotshot cop, or so Stetson had told me. Not needing any more officers, the neighboring town had offered him to Blaze, who had accepted, since he and Stetson were getting a bit overrun with crime lately.

Over a midnight supper of pancakes, sunny-side-up eggs, bacon, and a bowl of strawberries with fresh cream, Stetson filled me in on what he knew about the case. It wasn't much more than what I already knew, though it did take Jamie and a few other people off my list, including Jeff. I'd never suspected the kind doctor, even though Mabel had, but it was still a relief to know he was innocent.

Unlike Blaze, Stetson saw me as a friend, and he had no problem not treating me like a cow at an auction. He was the main reason I had stayed up so late. We'd talked for over an hour, and if it were another universe, I could see myself liking Stetson as more than a friend.

His tanned face was angular, lips almost always stretched in a grin, and he had a contagious laugh. Except for the slight bump on the bridge of his nose and the faint scar by his hair-line, I almost couldn't tell that he had once been a bull rider before settling down into small-town police work. He wore his black hair a bit longer than Blaze did, and it always had a hat band dent in the back, matching the tan line that went across his forehead.

For as long as I'd known him, Stetson had had his eyes on Misty, though he'd dated Lacey for a few months the first year I lived in Flamingo Springs. For whatever reason, even though Misty liked him back, they'd never gotten together. It'd been nice to catch up with him, listening to his stories about what was going on out at his ranch where he raised a few head of cattle.

Now, as he stood talking to Kasey and Mitch while Brey

sighed over her new beau, I thought back to what the quiet cowboy had told me the night before concerning Blaze. "He's a good guy, Aubrey," he'd said. "But Blaze is a bit like my favorite mustang. Stubborn, headstrong, and it's his way or nothing. Don't let him bother you."

"Easier said than done," I grumbled under my breath as I spotted the sheriff in question strolling down the street. Looking clean cut as always, hat firmly settled on his head, Blaze made his way down the sidewalk, taking in the flurry of activity that surrounded him. Cars lined the street as tourists poured in, eager to grab breakfast at the hotel, which was the only place in town that was open.

Seeing how many people were swarming the streets, I knew the sizeable load of food I'd sent over earlier was probably already gone. Brey and I had already turned more than a dozen people away, letting them know we were closed for the day, but if they headed out to Cody's, they'd be able to buy my wares after eight.

Darting back into the diner, I hefted another box of goodies. Brey ticked things off the list we'd compiled the night before, and the sweet smell of glazed cinnamon rolls tickled my nose. Sliding the box into my vehicle, I stood back, listening to Brey as she read the list, wiping sweat away from my eyes. From sweets to plain, homemade bread that I served with either honey butter or cinnamon butter, to lemonade, iced tea, and business cards, it sounded like we'd packed the entire store into my Jeep.

This was my third Fourth of July in Flamingo Springs, second as an official store owner, and Brey's second year doing it with me. I knew she loved it. From the grin on her face, this year would probably go down in her books as the best ever since Kasey was attending.

Two doors down, I heard Brent help organize a line for loading up Jeni's jewelry supplies, and looking the other way, I could make out Suzanne helping Jesse load his truck. Vincent and Marie were scurrying around the front of their restaurant, Marie flapping her arms in the air like she wanted to take flight while Vincent shouted something I couldn't make out. But when they both started laughing, I smiled.

The Fourth can be a stressful time. Remembering what it's about, I relaxed my shoulders and checked my watch. "Time to hit the road," I told Brey. "Are you riding with me, or do you want to hitch one with Mitch and Kasey?"

Shoving her apron in the back of my Jeep, she gave me a big smile. "I'm gonna go over with them." She took off toward Kasey, who was filming the activity on the street, Stetson nowhere to be seen, but turned back, blond hair shiny in the sunlight, clear eyes bright. "If that's okay with you ..." she trailed off.

I only laughed, shaking my head. "Yeah, go ahead. I've got this. As long as you show up fifteen minutes before we start, I'm good." I waved her off as I headed back into the diner to make one final round, making sure I had everything I needed. Stopping by the bathroom, I peered into the mirror, smoothing a few errant strands of hair away from my face. I'd gone with an all cowgirl look for the day, donning a snug, knee-length jean skirt paired with cowboy boots that were showing a bit of wear. A white tank top peeked out from the open throated purple plaid shirt I wore, and I'd completed the look with a big turquoise belt and blue feather earrings that almost reached my shoulders. I'd put my hair back a tight French braid, and for a moment, it was like I'd lived in Texas my whole life and hadn't lived in New York City just a few short years ago.

Clicking off the light, I headed outside, locking the door behind me. The sound of engines revving filled the air as vendors started the twenty-minute drive to Cody's. I waved at Brey as she hung out the back-passenger window of Mitch's Humvee. Kasey sat next to her while Misty claimed the front seat next to Mitch, pink hair floating around her face as she said something to the internet star, who was laughing.

She'd help Brey and me if we needed it, as would Mabel, who went flying by in her little red car, clearly eager to get the day started. Once my stand was closed for the day, or sold out, whichever came first, we'd stuff ourselves on all the goodies laid out. After Brent finished the short sermon he was always asked to give on the Fourth, we'd make our way to the rodeo ring to watch cowboys try their hand at roping and bull riding.

"Be gentle with those!" I heard Jeni shrill at Mike as he helped her load a few final boxes. Even from across the street I could see the grin that stretched across his features, the widower enjoying poking fun at the jewelry maker. I waved as Jamie drove past with her husband and multiple kids, the trunk of her low-riding mini-van packed with boxes of designer clothing.

Hearing a clatter, I turned to watch Lacey as she struggled over her threshold with a suitcase, leaving to spend the weekend with her mother as she did every year. When she turned her Texas smile on Blaze as he took it from her and loaded it into her small car, I hopped up into my Jeep and cranked the engine to life. He'd been making his rounds all morning, helping everyone on the street with something, except me.

Nose tilted in the air, I slid my sunglasses on. Men. Shifting gears, I eased out onto the street and headed toward Cody's, pulling the sun visor down once I hit blacktop, the glare of the sun almost blinding. Heat waves danced and shimmied their way across the road in front of me. I turned on the radio and caught the weather, pleased to hear that it was going to be mostly sunny with highs in the mid 90s. It'd be a bit cooler at Cody's since he had a lot of shade trees, but the hotter it was, the better my drinks sold. I could almost feel my wallet getting fatter.

For events like these, I usually paid Brey double time, but for today, I was going to give her triple time. She deserved it. My waitress put up with a lot from me, Terri, Mabel, and even Misty, and I never wanted her to think she wasn't appreciated.

Cranking up the AC, I squinted into the sunlight as patriotic country music blasted from the speakers. Leaving the small desert Flamingo Springs resided in and entering the green plains that signified I was entering Jackson territory, I relaxed. Despite the criticism I've thrown at Cody, I can testify that if there's one thing about his ranch I love, it's how comfortable it is. As soon as visitors drive through the gate—with a cow skull attached to the top of it, they feel like they've come home, and I think that's why the Fourth has become such a success.

Gravel crunched under my tires as I eased into a parking spot. Vendors milled around, carrying supplies across the driveway to the side yard that was set up for us. Cody's sprawling ranch home has a yard the size of a national park, and he reserved half of the front for parking and the other half for vendors. The back was set up for the buffet and bonfire, and beyond that lay the barns and their various fenced-off sections, the cows having been relocated to a southern pasture for the day.

The cowboy star himself came down the drive to greet me, opening the back gate of my Jeep after dazzling me with a grin. He took an appreciative sniff of a box before picking it up. "I swear, Aubrey, every time you bring stuff to an event I think you've brought too much, and you always prove me wrong by selling out in only a few hours."

Grabbing another box after pocketing my keys, I fell in step next to him. "Tell me about it. I have enough food here to feed at least five hundred people, but send a few of your ranch hands through the line, and it'll be enough for about a hundred."

Cody laughed, the spurs on his worn boots jingling as he

strode toward a green-and-white striped booth that had my name painted across the top. It looked just like the ones you see at a fair, only a bit bigger, and was lined up next to several smaller ones that looped around to make a horseshoe. "That's 'cause you're the best, Aubrey." He set the box on the front counter, and I followed suit.

Opening the side door, he beckoned me to follow him in. Once we were inside, he showed me a small panel on the back wall, the sudden index of heat slapping me in the face as the sounds of activity outside hummed around us. "You and Jesse have electricity this year, so you don't have to worry about sending someone to buy ice every ten minutes." He clicked a switch on and moved past me to touch the metal countertop the boxes sat on. The bright sunlight outside made it hard to see inside, even though there was an overhead light.

"I've got cooling lines that run under the counter, and an AC unit that'll blow on everything." He turned and gave me a grin. "Promise me a batch of white chocolate raspberry scones sometime, and I'll knock the vending price down to fifty dollars."

I considered his offer. To be a vendor at Cody's you had to pay three hundred dollars, plus an insurance deposit, so he was taking a loss with his offer. I nodded. "I'll take it." I looked around, appreciating the new flooring and shelves that had been installed since last year, taking in a deep breath of sawdust, dirt, and the light aftershave that wafted from Cody. "You did a lot of work in this. I like it."

"Thanks," he said. "I know last year you had to just use a lot of ice and about thirty fans, so I thought I'd be a nice guy and install AC. I did the same for Jesse and was almost done with Vicki's before, well ..." His face darkened as he trailed off. "Before she passed."

"You're a good guy, Cody Jackson." I patted his hand that still stretched out on the counter, eyeing the metal shelves, that, before long, would be filled with sweets. Shoppers could eye them through a glass window that slid to the side much like the windows at the drive-thrus of fast-food establishments. "Now let's go get the rest of my stuff before it melts!"

I decided against giving him a piece of my mind about how he'd mischievously misled Blaze, since he was clearly offering me an apology by lowering my booth price. Despite all his joking ways, Cody had a good heart, and once again, I found myself doubting he was capable of murder.

The following half hour was a slew of running back and forth to my car, barking orders at Brey and two of the men who worked for Cody. By the time we were finished setting up and were in the final ten minutes before the day officially began, my boots had little pools of sweat in them. I'd stripped to my tank top, deciding I'd put my plaid shirt back on once evening fell.

"Good night," Brey exclaimed, out of breath after gulping down half a bottle of water. "I'm about to melt."

Turning my face toward one of the fans, I let the cold air dry my sweaty face, taking a deep whiff of the smell of sweets it whirled around the small shack. "Same here. Thank God for Cody installing AC this year."

Brey started to say something else but was cut off when a roar went up outside. Looking out the window, we saw that a large truck had pulled up, and two very well-known and liked celebrities climbed out of it. I grinned while Brey gasped, scrambling around to find some paper and a pen before shoving past me to go outside and join the crowd. The two pop singers were good friends of almost everyone in town, and I'd had them sit in my living room more than once. Though they were always seen together, and it was rumored they were an item, they really weren't. From the way Jeni was beating a path from her stand to the truck, a bright smile on her pink lips, it was obvious she'd heard the same thing.

They handled the crowd like pros, signing autographs and

posing for selfies while answering questions, and only when the next vehicle of stars arrived did they get a break. The newcomers, unlike the pop singers, who were clad in jeans, sneakers, and ballcaps, were decked out in Hollywood's idea of cowboy attire. They had enough silver on their boots and belts to signal the space station, and the tasseled, gaudy shirts they wore weren't much better. Feathered, rhinestoned hats adorned their heads, and they greeted the crowd with loud yee-haw yells.

I chuckled as I watched people run around. Being star struck could happen to anyone. A middle-aged mom with her husband and kids in tow a grandpa right behind them as he waved a piece of paper in the air were living proof. Chants echoed across the dry air as the celebrities twirled for their adoring fans while the two singers hugged Brent and Suzanne, two of their closest friends.

Blaze had finally arrived and stood off to the side, arms crossed over his chest, legs spread wide, a lone figure standing out from the crowd. Even with the distance that separated us, I could see a grin teasing his lips, and when Stetson approached him, the new assistant officer safely holed up in the office in town, Blaze threw back his head and laughed, the rich sound carrying over to me above the noise of the crowd. He said something back to Stetson, though his deputy was already craning his neck, having spotted Misty's pink hair in the distance as she walked with Mitch, pointing out a few things of interest to him.

"Ladies and gentlemen, if I could grab y'all's attention for just a minute!" Cody's voice rang out above the heavy din of the crowd, and everyone fell silent, facing him. He'd taken up residence on top of Jesse's stand, which was across and down a bit from mine and was the sturdiest of them all. He propped his hands on his hips and surveyed everyone for a moment before continuing, his lean frame cutting a sharp figure against the blue sky. Apparently, I wasn't the only one thinking that, because a few women let out catcalls while another let out a loud wolf whistle.

Cody raised his hands, and I slid the serving window open a crack so I could hear him better, scanning the crowd for Brey as I did so. "Thank you, ladies. Thank you." He grinned. "My name is Cody Jackson, and I'm the owner of Jackson Ranch." He paused. "A couple of y'all are already looking a bit pink, so I'll keep this short, so you can go buy something to drink." The crowd laughed, and he continued. "This is the fifth year Jackson Ranch has hosted a Fourth of July bash, and to everyone who's been here before, thanks for coming back. If this is your first time, I just wanna extend a big welcome to the family." He put his hands back on his hips, the broad brim of his hat shielding his face, and I shivered as my shirt started drying in the cold air blowing on my back.

"Now, today is Independence Day, a day where we not only remember what happened all them hundreds of years ago, but we also remember those who have served to make sure we get to celebrate. We're patriots down here in Texas, and we just ask that if you decide to get into a discussion of politics, that you keep it civil."

A loud round of applause drowned his words out. He waited until the crowd had settled down before going on. "We're gonna open the stands in about three minutes, and up until noon, you can shop to your heart's desire and get to know us residents of Flamingo Springs. After that, the stands are closed, and lunch will be laid out in the back yard. It's a thirty-dollar fee, but there's no limit to how much you can eat, and that also covers the bonfire later. You can buy your tickets at the booth I'm currently standing on, and kids under four eat for free."

He pointed to where Pastor Brent stood off to the side. "After lunch, Pastor Brent is going to bless us with a short sermon, and then we've got plenty of entertainment and games. We've got some bull riding going on around four, and since we support our military and our brothers and sisters who wear blue, we also ask that you consider donating a small amount at some point today. All proceeds from the donations go to charities around the country."

Starting to turn to jump off the booth, he turned back and said, "And one more thing. As you noticed, we've got a couple celebrities with us today. Now, they're no different from us except that they've got more money, so please just be considerate and treat them with respect and let them enjoy the day. Pastor Brent is gonna lead us in prayer to start today, and after that, the stands are open."

Jumping to the ground, he nodded at Brent, who stepped up in front of the booth. Deciding to not climb it, he stood still and led us in a simple prayer that asked for the Lord's blessing, protection, and goodwill. A heartfelt 'amen' went up when he was finished, and since it looked like much of the crowd was headed toward my stand, I slid the window open the rest of the way and slipped an apron over my head.

Brey darted in just as the first couple reached the window, and within minutes, we were selling sweets and breads faster than we could unpack them to the display counter. It got to the point where people just yelled out what they wanted and shoved money at me, not caring if they saw what the food they wanted looked like. Brey was so busy pouring tea and lemonade that she could only sway side to side to let me move past her, and by ten, we were out of drinks. By ten thirty, I was putting up the closed sign, having just sold the final donut to the two pop stars, who went off to split it. I didn't feel bad for them, though, because that was the fourth time they'd been to my booth.

Despite the steady whir of the AC unit, both Brey and myself had consumed several glasses of lemonade and were dripping with sweat, which is why we'd packed extra shirts and bottles of deodorant. Looking across the small path between us and Jesse, I saw that he was hard pressed to keep up with handing out the slushies he was selling, and leaning out across the counter to peer down the street, it looked like everyone else was making some serious money as well.

Digging through the cash drawer, I pulled out a wad of hundreds and counted out four before stuffing the rest back into the drawer and locking it. Reaching my hand under the counter, I slid it into the hideaway Cody had built for me and locked the little metal door, slipping the key into my pocket. Turning, I handed two of the hundreds to Brey, who was slamming down a warm bottle of water she'd found in her purse.

"What?" she gasped, looking at me in shock, but I just laughed and pressed the money into her hand.

"You're the best help a body could ask for, and you put up with a lot. Consider this a Fourth of July bonus. Now go blow it and have fun with Kasey."

She gave me a sweaty hug before bounding out of the stand to go fix her makeup in Cody's guest bathroom. One of the perks of being friends with the ranch owner was getting access to his house while the tourists and most other vendors had to make do with the porta-potties he had brought in.

Busying myself with stacking the empty totes in each other, I wiped everything down with alcohol wipes, ensuring that the stand was as clean as it had been before I had used it. Outside, the heavy buzz of activity bounced against the wooden sides of the shack. I smiled at the pleasant sound. The happy cries of children could be heard as they ran from stand to stand, eating their slushies and munching on the cheddar jalapeño popcorn Jesse was handing out for free. Low laughs and yee-haws echoed up and down the small street, and more than once I heard Mitch's excited voice as he walked around, filming everything he could, while Kasey asked people for interviews.

A sharp tap on the now closed window brought my head around, and I frowned when I saw it was Blaze. We'd avoided each other the past few days, and he'd kept his distance from the stand even when Stetson had trotted over to buy a few sweets. The trees that towered over the line of booths offered a bit of shade in the mid-morning light, but even in the shadows, I could see that Blaze's lips were pressed into a grim line.

Surprisingly enough, no one, not even Cody, had mentioned what had happened at Vicki's memorial, and though I was remorseful about my outburst, I was still irritated at Blaze. From the way he was glowering at me through the glass, it was clear he felt the same way.

Realizing I'd been staring at him and therefore was unable to ignore him, I crossed the booth in three steps and slid the window open. The gust of hot dry wind brought the smell of Jesse's popcorn to my nose, and my mouth watered. I wasn't sure what to expect from Blaze, so when he shoved a cold bottle of water at me, I was a little taken aback, though it didn't stop me from grabbing it.

"Thanks." I twisted the lid off and taking a good swig. "I think I've drank enough lemonade to last until next year."

Blaze eyed me. "These booths get pretty hot, and I didn't want to have to find Jeff if you keeled over from heat stroke."

That made sense. He'd brought me the water out of duty, not kindness, and not knowing how to answer, I took another drink. While serving hungry customers, Brey had watched Jeff attend to three different people who were struggling with the heat, and the last I'd seen him, he'd been chowing down a piece of pie that Vincent and Marie were selling, a happy grin stretching his tan features.

"Also, I figured you'd be hungry, so I picked you up some deep-fried cheese curds and chicken strips from that guy who comes up from Louisiana." Blaze pushed a cardboard hotdog box at me, and I looked at it for a long moment before glancing up at him.

"I don't like to hold grudges, Aubrey," he said softly, leaning on the counter with both forearms so that his head was partly in the booth. "And after a good long talk with the Lord and Stetson, I think I need to extend an apology for my behavior."

Up until a week ago, Blaze and I had only ever flirted with each other in passing. We'd mainly spent our time arguing, and nothing had brought him more joy than giving me a ticket. In the last week, we'd went from being courteous enemies to almost friends, and it didn't escape me the way his eyes dropped to my lips, as if he was currently remembering the kiss we'd shared only a few nights ago. I know I was, and at the moment, I wouldn't have minded repeating it.

Taking my silence for anger, he nudged the food toward me. "Peace offering?" he said, giving me a grin, and with a laugh, I nodded and picked it up. Slipping out the side door after closing the window and locking it, I joined him around front, handing him my water bottle after he locked the door so I could eat. As we strolled down the street, stopping at the stands to ooh and ahh over everything being offered, I couldn't help but notice the admiring looks he was getting from most of the women around us.

Jealousy tried to make itself known, but after I threw the empty food box away and wiped my hands, Blaze made it clear he only had eyes for one person when he grabbed my hand and held it tight, his dry palm warm against my slightly sweaty one. Looking down at me, he said, "Wanna go see what Jeni's sellin'?"

"Sure," I answered. "I've been eyeing some of her silver and turquoise pieces for a while. Maybe she's offering a deal." We headed toward Jeni's bright orange stand that looked a lot like the open manger Cody had built for Christmas last year, the sides of it lined with little black velvet shelves that held set after set of beautiful, handmade jewelry, much of which she made herself.

"Having fun?" I admired the way Blaze's hat threw his face in shadows, highlighting his lean jaw. Looking down at me, he flashed his dimples.

"I am now."

I blushed and stared at my feet, inhaling the scents of dust and sweet grass mixed with the smells of carnival food, the sun tracing a soothing pattern on my bare arms. I had no idea how to respond to such a compliment, and thankfully, I didn't have to worry about it, because he nudged my shoulder with his. "Is that Mabel?"

Looking up, I turned in the direction he pointed and saw a small clown making its way down the street, blowing bubbles at everyone as they laughed and took pictures. I say small clown because its body was the size of a child, but it was wearing stilts that brought its height up to a foot taller than Blaze, who brushed the six-foot three mark.

I laughed, getting a better look at the clown's face as we drew closer. "Yeah, I think it is." I popped a bubble as it floated past. "I didn't know she knew how to walk on stilts."

"Really?" Jesse said as he wandered up to us, offering me a bag of popcorn, which, of course I took. "She used to run a birthday party business back before she moved here. She was telling me about it one day when we were playing checkers." He sent me a teasing grin and I forced myself to meet his gaze, squelching down a bit of guilt.

"We used to talk a lot up until you moved here and became her favorite friend." He chuckled to take out the sting from his words and continued as Mabel drew closer, blowing kisses at kids as they pointed at her while their parents took pictures. "Back when she lived in Austin, she'd go to birthday parties and provide entertainment for the kids. Made quite a name for herself. I think she ran a small bakery on the side and provided the sweets for the parties."

He frowned, snitching a few kernels of popcorn from my bag and popping them into his mouth. "She did really good up until she hurt her back when she fell down the stairs in her house. After that, she said it was just too hard to keep doing it, so she moved here and became an insurance agent."

"I vaguely remember her mentioning her clown days when I first moved here," I said.

Blaze let out a noncommittal grunt, cutting me off, staring at the shopkeeper with an odd expression on his face. Looking at our hands, Jesse raised an eyebrow teasingly, but I shook my head.

"Thanks for the popcorn," I told him, trying to warn him from saying anything about the fact Blaze and I were apparently becoming an item.

"Yeah, sure, no problem," he said, winking. "I love my friends, and if giving them popcorn makes them happy, I'm all for it."

Knowing I had to tell Jesse what I'd done at some point, I winced. Blaze tugged me forward, clearly eager to get away from the grocery mart owner.

"Thanks," he said coolly. "That's great info."

Looking up at him, I saw that he was chewing on his lower lip and had a pensive look in his eyes. I looked at Jesse over my shoulder and gave a half shrug, then pulled on Blaze's arm. "Hey, earth to Blaze. You need some water?"

Blaze declined. "Nah, thanks, just thought of something I need to look into tomorrow, that's all." He looked down at me. "Sorry, I kinda drifted off for a minute."

I was about to tell him that yeah, he had, but by then Mabel was standing in front us. She grinned down at me with a big bright clown smile, her brown eyes dancing in a face that was covered in paint and glitter. A bright purple wig sat on her head, a jaunty black top hat perched on it, and the checkered pink and blue baggy shirt and pants she wore fluttered in the slight breeze. "Hiya, Aubrey!" she crowed, blowing bubbles down on us. "Whatcha think of my look?"

"I love it," I told her. "You mentioned you used to be a clown, but I didn't know you were so good at it."

"Yeah," Blaze echoed, sliding an arm around my waist, causing the young woman who'd been beelining for him to veer off course and head for Stetson, who looked around like he was about run.

The woman latched onto Stetson's arm, and I turned my attention back to Mabel. "What made you dress up today?"

Mabel shrugged. "Oh, I don't know. Feeling a bit nostalgic, I think. I was digging through some boxes the other week and decided I wanted to see if I still have the touch." She paused and leaned down to pat a kid's head as he waved up at her, giving a big grin to the phone his mom was holding up.

"However," she groaned, rubbing her back, "I think I'm about done. Ever since I fell, my back just can't handle the pressure of being on stilts for more than an hour."

"I can imagine," Blaze said sympathetically, still holding me close, and despite it being hot outside, I didn't mind being close to him. In fact, I was basking in the feel of his strong arm looped around my waist and being pressed into his side. For the first time in years, I knew I'd met someone I could trust completely, and the thought made me rest my head on his shoulder.

He started to say something else but was interrupted when Mabel let out a shriek and took a hard swing at the hornet buzzing her wig. The movement threw her off balance and sent her toward the ground. Before I could blink, Blaze jumped forward to grab her, his hat almost falling off as he did so. Amidst the cheers of nearby onlookers, he steadied Mabel and handed her wig back, dusting it off after scooping it up from the ground.

"My lands," Mabel gasped reaching out for me. "I think that's it. I'm done being on stilts. Though this and baking are my two great loves, I'm gonna have to let this one go." I led her over to a bench that was situated between two stands, the trip to Jeni's momentarily forgotten as I helped her take the stilts off and fetched her a bottle of soda, which she quickly guzzled.

I looked around for Blaze as Mabel slid on her normal shoes after pulling them from a big pocket in her pants. Being so small, the shoes she wore on the stilts were only around a women's size ten, anything bigger would have thrown her off balance too much. I fingered the red string on them as she caught her breath, cracking jokes left and right. I noticed that part of the blue inside of her right shoe was stained a bright red that matched Jamie's dyed hair, as if she'd worn a sock that had bled quite a bit.

Before I could ask her about it, Blaze reappeared, and though he tried to hide it, I could see that he was worried. Looking over my shoulder, I saw that Stetson was as well, Blaze having clearly talked to him, but when I looked at the tall sheriff, he only shook his head. He told Mabel to be careful before helping her to her feet and sending her off toward Misty and Mitch who were roaming past, laughing at the giant ice cone they were sharing.

"Aubrey." Blaze took my hand, pulling me toward Jeni, who was grinning at me while holding out the earrings I'd been coveting for over a year. "Do me a favor and don't go anywhere by yourself today."

He looked down at me when I stopped.

"What's going on?" I asked him, nerves starting to dance in my stomach. "What are you talking about?"

He smiled, as if doing his best to ease my worries. "Could be something. Could be nothing. Just promise me you won't go off on your own."

Agreeing, I moved forward, digging in my pocket for money, Jeni bagging the earrings up. Something was off, that much was obvious, and if Blaze thought I was in danger, the best thing I could do was pretend I didn't know I was.

My throat worked as we started back down the street, our fingers intertwined together as townspeople raised their eyebrows and grinned at me. My life wasn't the only thing in danger right now. My heart was, too, and while I'd fight to keep the former, I wasn't so sure I would for the latter.

11

S kirt feeling tight, I wondered if I could handle another slice of tender pork. It was a little after one, and everyone was gathered in Cody's several-acre backyard, seated on benches and chairs beneath large trees. The food was lined up on tables under canopies, fans blowing across everything to keep the flies away. The containers that held the cold food were seated in inflatable swimming pools filled with ice, the crockpots holding the hot food plugged into extension cords. The sweet and smoky scents of barbecue, beans, fruit, and every other food you could imagine wafted through the air, and beside me, Blaze let out a satisfied sigh, having packed back around four plates of food.

We'd found chairs next to Misty and Mitch, Kasey and Brey seated to our left, and had laughed and joked as we'd devoured the food, Cody making his rounds every so often to make sure everyone was happy. The tourists seated behind us had turned out to be quite nice and entertained us with hilarious stories of fishing up in Wisconsin. The husband struck up a conversation with Blaze, as the man was a retired fire fighter.

Misty grinned at me as she wiped flecks of barbecue sauce off her lips with a red and white checkered paper napkin, green eyes twinkling. "I think I eat enough on the Fourth to feed a small army," she chuckled, pushing a hand through the pink hair that escaped the bun on top of her head. "And lemonade, my stars! I think my blood is starting to crystalize from all the sugar."

Nodding, I let out a groan, still thinking about the pork. "Tell me about it. But within an hour, we'll be back for more."

Mitch leaned around Misty and sent me a thumbs up. "If this is what it's like living in Texas, sign me up! I'd move here tomorrow if it meant food like this all the time."

"You telling me you L.A. boys don't have pig roasts?" Grinning, I leaned back in my chair, crossing my legs.

"Are you kidding?" Kasey piped up from where he and Brey were sharing a large slice of sweet watermelon that she was currently doctoring with salt. "A tofu roast, maybe."

"Are you going to try your hand in the roping ring?" I asked the two stars, glancing across the clearing everyone was circled about, which would later host the bonfire. Here and there I spotted a few celebrities, clearly having the time of their lives as they ate with the peace of knowing there wasn't any paparazzi around to accuse them of being fat.

"I think I might," Mitch said, but Kasey only moaned.

"I'd throw up," he said. "You guys might have to roll me around if I don't stop eating soon."

Brey swatted his arm. "Well don't quit yet. I can't finish this fruit on my own."

Misty and I shared a grin, both knowing full well my waitress could eat an entire watermelon if she so desired. Taking one last sip of her drink, Misty stood. "I'm going for some water," she said. "Aubrey, wanna come with?"

The look she sent me offered no room for refusal, so I got

up from my chair. Blaze dropped his hand away from my knee where it'd been resting for the last half hour, and I obediently followed her across the yard to the tent that housed dozens of different beverages.

"What?" I asked, tossing my plate into the large trash bin as she poured a glass of water.

"You and Blaze seemed to have worked things out." She lifted an eyebrow at me. "What's up with that?"

I shrugged, studying the grass beneath the table. "If I knew, I'd tell you."

She shook her head. "Looks like I was right about him after all." She sent me a wicked grin. "And I have to say, you two look perfect together. Like two little peas in a pod."

"Oh, shut up," I growled playfully, slugging her in the arm as she drank from her cup, the result spilling the water down the front of her gray T-shirt and pink shorts.

A whistle sounded outside, and we grinned at each other. "Wanna abandon the guys and go watch the cowboys do what they do best?" She threw her cup in the trash, then smoothed down her shirt.

"You have to ask?" I replied as Brey and Mabel appeared in the tent, clearly having the same idea.

"Kasey is sweet and all," Brey said in a low voice, taking a moment to check her makeup in the selfie mode of her phone, "but when it comes to the rodeo ring, I don't want no man with me, 'cause I wanna cheer for whoever's the cutest."

"Same." Misty and I grinned at each other, Mabel echoing our sentiments. We left the tent and made our way toward the large fenced-in ring Cody kept set up by one of the barns. Like everyone else heading that way, it wasn't long before we started sweating, our legs heavy with the extra weight of all the food we'd consumed, and even Misty was breathing hard and fanning herself by the time we got to the ring.

We bypassed the small bleachers that had been erected and gathered around the fence, wrapping our hands around the metal poles as we watched Cody's ranch hands get ready for the roping competition. Mabel let out a cat call as one of them walked by, clad in jeans and chaps with a tucked in T-shirt, holding a rope in one hand. He tipped the brim of his hat toward her, and she squealed.

Once a big enough crowd had gathered, filling the bleachers and the lawn chairs, cowboys wove their way through the mass, holding out their hats, which were quickly filled as people eagerly donated to support the various charities. Reaching into our pockets, Misty, Brey, Mabel and I all chucked in a couple of twenties, and Brant, the cowboy whose hat we'd put the money into, gave us a bow, grinning, before moving toward the tourists behind us.

"Y'all ready for a good time?" Cody yelled, climbing up and sitting on top of a fence post, looking down on everyone. At the roar that met his question, he laughed and jumped into the ring, spurs jingling when his boots struck the dirt. He headed toward a gate that led to smaller compartments, which held horses and bulls. A cowboy sat on a restless horse behind it. Grabbing onto the latch, Cody nodded at one of his ranch hands, who held a chute shut. Giving a countdown, they opened the gates and let a heifer out, and the games began.

Cowboy after cowboy tried his hand at roping, while Cody kept score with a whiteboard. After he took his turn and won second place, the ring was opened to the kids, who were taught a few tricks and how to rope a saddle. Cody kept the jokes flowing and the crowd laughing as he showed kid after kid how to rope the fake steer. When one little girl fell and skinned her knee, he quickly picked her up and coaxed a smile out of her, plopping his hat on her head.

After that, it was time for the bull riding. It didn't surprise me to see Stetson and Blaze lined up to try their luck, having thrown in their seventy-five dollars to enter. Both ran ranches and had been part of the rodeo scene at one time. Going first, after handing his utility belt to Stetson, Blaze set a score of eighty-four. When Stetson went up, he wasn't far behind. Every single one of the men who worked for Cody had their chance, and since the Fourth at Cody's was, in a way, a small rodeo, several full-time bull riders showed up as well.

Cody was the last cowboy to go. I studied him as he sat astride the bull who had the unfortunate but very fitting name of Back Biter, biting down on his mouthpiece as Brant held the chute closed. The sun shone down on him, glinting in his blond hair as he nodded at something Stetson said. Even non-fans of the rodeo world who had no knowledge of bull riding could easy to tell that Cody was used to doing this. When the gate opened, it was clear he was king of the ring, and he had no trouble beating out Blaze's score.

"I get now why he's got all them belts," Mabel said, having never stayed around for this part of the Fourth before. "He's good."

I nodded, not taking my eyes off the fine figure Cody cut in the ring as he bowed to the screaming crowd. After a brief struggle, the bull was wrangled back into its pen. "I've watched him a few times on TV. It's crazy how good he is. He always comes in pretty high up on the scoreboard, and I know a lot of people bet on him."

"It'll catch up to him one day." Mabel sounded a bit sad. Seeing the puzzled expression on my face, she explained, "You can only tempt fate so many times before it lets you have it, and I just worry that one day we'll hear he got stomped by a bull or kicked in the head by a horse."

Not willing to tell Mabel he'd been hurt pretty badly a few times already, I looked back at Cody. His happy-go-lucky grin lit up his face, and though I knew I still needed to investigate him at some point, I struggled to believe that the handsome and energetic rancher could be capable of murder.

I had no words to give Mabel, who had been spouting depressing phrases all day. Turning back, I saw that Blaze was staring at us. The worry on his face was undeniable, but about what, I had no idea. When Kasey asked me for an interview and dared me to cat call Cody for the camera, I forgot to ask Blaze what was wrong, and proceeded to do the stupidest thing of my life. Ignore my gut.

ALL GOOD THINGS must come to an end. After several rounds of horseshoes and tug-of-war, I found myself seated on a grassy patch of ground next to Blaze, both of us leaning back on our hands as we watched fireworks explode above us. The bonfire had been a success, as it always was, and, resting my head on Blaze's shoulder, I breathed in the warm scent of smoke, barbecue, and aftershave, along with faint hints of leather and gun oil. All around us people gasped and pointed at the majestic display of color that bloomed in the sky, taking pictures and selfies. I heard Misty's laugh as she sat with Jeni and Marie, while Vincent and Jesse discussed the many different varieties of pesto behind them.

Stetson was somewhere off to our right, talking to one of the popstars, and for a moment, it was hard to concentrate on the show above me with so much noise around. But when Blaze's hand found mine, it was as if the world shrank, and it was just him and me. He'd taken his hat off and set it on the ground next to his feet. I could sense his eyes tracing my face as I looked up at the sky.

Knowing that if I turned to him, he'd kiss me, my stomach jumped. He breathed my name in-between booms, and I turned toward him, feeling like the air had been sucked out of my lungs. When warm lips met mine and lingered, the tension left my shoulders. Behind my eyelids, I could see flashes of brightness as the finale started. Blaze curled his fingers over mine and I felt him smile against my lips. I memorized the moment, tucking every detail of him—the way he smelled, how he tasted, the gentle way he was kissing me—deep inside my heart.

With one last boom, the fireworks ended, and pulling just far enough away so that he could speak, Blaze whispered, lips brushing mine, "Wow."

I gazed at him, feeling a bit dazed, and the only words that came to mind were, "Wow, indeed."

He chuckled, pressing one last kiss to my lips before pulling me to my feet. It was only once we were standing that I smelled something other than the sulfur from the fireworks. Just as it registered what I was smelling, a cry came from one of the barns that were private-access only, where Cody's expensive ranch equipment was stored.

"Fire! Fire in the south barn," someone yelled.

I ran after Blaze as he followed Cody. The rest of the crowd remained behind, Stetson instructing them to stay put until we knew what was going on. I coughed as an odd smelling smoke filled my throat and lungs. Blaze darted into the barn, Cody right behind him, but before anyone could even start the water hose or start to worry, they reemerged. Blaze looked angry in the beam of the flashlight one of the ranch hands held.

"What is it?" I asked, and he shook his head. "Some bits of hay caught on fire, and it spread to a few other things before dying out. No damage done, except to his reputation, which will be ruined when I haul him away for the possession and growing of illegal substances and hiding a blood-stained rolling pin behind them." He jerked his head toward where Cody stood off to the side talking to Stetson, waving his hands in the air, though I couldn't make out what he said.

"Don't tell me you believe those are his?" I gasped, following Blaze as he stomped toward Cody. "No way would he do that! And you've got to be kidding me thinking he killed Vicki!"

Blaze whirled and grabbed my shoulders. "Kinda hard to deny the six pots of marijuana growing under a sunlamp in there, one of which exploded and caused the fire, Aubrey. Kinda hard to ignore a blood-splattered murder weapon that fits the crime as perfectly as Cinderella's shoe."

Cody heard his words and turned. "Look, Blaze, you gotta believe me. I didn't kill Vicki! I've got an alibi, and you know it. I hadn't even seen her during the week before she was killed, and I don't know how those plants got in there. I don't even use that barn in the summer, and how it got unlocked is beyond me."

"It doesn't matter what I believe," Blaze bit out, letting me go and facing Cody. "What matters is the overwhelming evidence sitting in that barn." He pulled a set of zip ties from his belt while Stetson shooed people away from the barn. "Cody Jackson, you have the right to remain silent. You have the right—"

"Wait!" I burst in, grabbing Blaze's arm and stopping him from finishing.

"Blaze, don't do this. This'll ruin him." My voice was pleading as I fought to hold him back, but he only dragged me along with him.

"If he didn't want to be ruined, he shouldn't have been growing illegal substances," he snapped. "Now back off before I have to arrest you, too, for hindering me!"

He shook me off, but I jumped in front of him. "Blaze, think about it. Why would Cody sacrifice everything he has just for some weed? Why would he hold onto the murder weapon instead of getting rid of it? It doesn't make sense. You know he didn't do it." Blaze moved around me and started binding Cody's hands, but I grabbed him, halting his process. "Blaze, please, don't do this." I glanced at Cody, who's chin was set, his jaw so tight it twitched, and beyond the arrogance in his face, I saw fear, because he knew what being arrested would do to him.

"You do this, and you'll ruin him," I warned Blaze. "Even once he's proven innocent, his career will be over. No sponsor will work with him because of this. You know that. How do you know someone didn't plant the rolling pin, and that one of his ranch hands isn't growing the weed? If you won't listen, at least let everyone leave before you do it."

Looking into my eyes, Blaze let out a sigh and nodded to Stetson, who cut the ties off Cody. "Send your guests home," he said, "and then you're coming with us. I won't put on the report what for yet," he added, emphasizing the last word, "but don't hold your breath."

Cody nodded. "Thanks," he said quietly, and looking up into his face, I saw that the tall cowboy was white beneath his tan, and his eyes were glinting with tears over what he might lose. He walked away, Stetson sticking close to him, and once he bid everyone good night, posing for a few last pictures and hugging a few more kids, Blaze turned to me.

"I can't believe you," I hissed at him, being careful to keep my voice low so that no one could overhear us. "Seriously? Even I know you can't just arrest him like that."

Blaze sighed and held up a hand. "Aubrey, there's things going on you don't know about." He scowled. "And don't quote the law at me." He bent so that his lips brushed my ear. "Despite what you think, I'm not an idiot. I know Cody isn't growing weed, and I know he didn't kill Vicki. His alibi is too strong, but he doesn't need to know that. If I'm going to catch who's behind all this, they need to think I've closed the case and charged Cody with everything. That's clearly what they want to happen, so why not make them think it has?"

Blaze pulled back as Cody and Stetson rejoined us, and

looking past them, I saw that only Misty, Mabel, Kasey, Mitch, and Brey were left, everyone else heading home. "Trust me, I know what would happen if he got charged, so I'll make sure the documents never get scanned in. Don't worry. I got this."

Eyes meeting, he touched my chin, and before I could stop myself, I blurted out, "Do you think this case will ever actually will be closed? It just feels like we're running around without finding any type of answer, and every day, everything's just getting worse."

Blaze looked at me, Stetson stopping Cody from making a call on the cellphone he'd just pulled from his pocket. Giving a low laugh, he said, "Well, not everything." He let his words trail off, his tone heavy, and I blushed.

"These things take time, Aubrey, but you have to trust me when I tell you that Stetson and I are doing everything we can to figure this out, and part of tying up some of the loose ends is by doing this." Reaching in his pocket, Blaze brought out another pair of zip ties and approached Cody.

"Cody Jackson, due to the illegal substances found on your property, a weapon believed to have been used to carry out a deadly crime, your relationship with the deceased, and the discrepancies the Flamingo Springs Sheriff's Office has found in your alibi and your witness statement, you are being placed under arrest for the murder of Victoria Phillips. You know your rights and will receive everything you are legally required to as soon as we arrive at the jail."

Now that there was no crowd around to bear witness to his arrest, only ranch hands and friends, Cody had no issue fighting back and he yelled, jerking away as Blaze reached for his wrists, "You have got to be kidding me, Blaze. You're arresting me based on some false facts and planted drugs?" He stepped away but was stopped when Stetson took a firm hold of his arm and whispered something in his ear, the last bit sounding like "The right to use force if you resist."

Cody dropped his head. "I want a lawyer," he said, "and once I get one, I'm suing you for everything you've got on grounds of false accusation and false imprisonment." He shoved away from Stetson, but allowed Blaze to tie his wrists. As they started to walk him away, he looked back over his shoulder, his voice hoarse, from tears or smoke I couldn't tell. "You better think twice about having Hotshot as your boyfriend," he sneered, "'cause it seems to me that if he don't like you, he's gonna pin a crime on you whether or not you did it."

He started to say something else, but a sharp word from Blaze silenced him, and I was left standing by the barn that still had a few wisps of smoke lingering around it. Ranch hands scurried about, trying to figure out what to do since their boss had just been arrested, and the chill that swept over me had me hurrying toward Misty. Her face was lit up by her cell phone screen as she texted someone, and I knew that before morning, everyone in Flamingo Springs would know that Cody had been implemented in Vicki's murder.

Letting out a frustrated sigh, I started the drive home. I just wished Blaze would tell me what was going on under that hat.

Making my way up to my apartment, I no longer had the urge to be nervous or to look over my shoulder like I had on previous nights, because common sense said that if Cody was in jail on murder charges, the real killer wouldn't need to try anything else. Someone else was taking the rap for the crimes, and the killer would get off completely free. As far as they were concerned, the case was closed, and no one would ever be the wiser to what they had done, and what they had tried to do to me.

Breathing out a thankful prayer, I knew I was safe for the first time in a week. Even as I showered the day's grime off and climbed into bed, a small voice in the back of my head wondered if maybe, just maybe, the threat of danger was even greater now. I squished the thought and rolled over, but as I drifted off to sleep a tinge of fear balled up in my stomach and sat like a two-ton bull.

This case wasn't over yet, and only God knew who else would get hurt.

"Yes, Lacey," I said into my cell phone as I loaded my dishwasher, wiping my damp hands with a dish towel after I put in a pod of soap and started it. "I was there, remember? That's how you found out that he was arrested."

"I know. I know," Lacey sobbed into my ear, having just returned from Houston. "But I just can't believe he murdered her. I had no idea Cody was capable of something like that."

"Look," I said, holding the phone to my ear with my shoulder as I sat on my couch and pulled on ankle socks, "he's only been arrested on the allegation of murder. Formally, he hasn't been charged with anything yet."

"Yet," Lacey cried. "Oh, Aubrey, why do I always pick the worst men?"

Remaining quiet, I wasn't sure she wanted me to answer that one, and when she'd managed to stop hiccupping, she said, "Can anyone post his bail yet?"

"I don't think that right now that would be a wise decision," I finally said, rolling my eyes. "If Cody is the killer, he's exactly where he needs to be."

"And if he's not?" Lacey challenged, and I sighed.

"Then we need to trust Blaze and Stetson with this."

After a few more words of encouragement and common sense, I got off the phone and took a moment to just stare into space, holding a sneaker in my hand. For some reason, since people had seen Blaze and I get cozy at the Fourth of July party, they all assumed I had some sort of inside scoop they didn't. Since Blaze wasn't taking any questions, everyone was coming to me. Marie, Jeff, and Jeni had all called me in the forty-five minutes I'd been up. I mean, they weren't wrong thinking that I knew something, but if Blaze wasn't talking, why would I?

I finished lacing my shoes and headed for the door. I needed a vacation. Mabel had been texting Misty and me pictures of Hawaii since six, and I had to admit the thought of a girls' vacation to a tropical island was very appealing, and it was getting more so with every passing minute. Mabel said she could get us cheap tickets, and if we shared a room, it would be affordable.

Stepping out onto my landing, I pocketed my keys, but just before headed down the stairs, I thought I heard a crash come from inside. I unlocked the door, and rushed back in. Everything looked fine until I went into the bathroom and saw that the mirror that had been mounted to the wall had pulled its nails right out of the wood and hit the floor, shattering all over the green bathmat.

Staring at where the mirror had once been, I tried to figure out how on earth that could have even happened, but after a moment's time, I realized I had only twenty minutes until Brey was expecting me to join her in the diner. I set to work, sweeping up the bits of glass and vacuuming the rug, leaning the empty frame against the tub wall to be dealt with when I got home. By the time I finished, I had lost ten minutes. I went back outside and pulled the door shut. It wasn't until I heard it click that I remembered I'd left my keys on the kitchen counter. I groaned. I didn't have a spare, so that meant calling for help, so I turned and raised my foot to step down on the top step.

"Aubrey! Aubrey stop!" Stetson's voice cracked through the air like the whip of a cowboy herding livestock, and I froze, holding onto the rail with one hand, the other clutching my phone while my foot hung suspended in the air. "Whatever you do," Stetson said, his voice closer now, "do not take that step."

Looking over the rail, I saw him standing by the edge of my building looking up at me, hazel eyes shielded by the shadow of his hat brim, but there was no missing the twist of his lips, nor the anxiety in his voice. "What is it?" my voice quavered down at him, thinking there was a gator on the steps below me, though considering the part of Texas we lived in, that was highly unlikely.

Stetson took a step forward. "You need to go back inside," he said, but I shook my head.

"I can't," I told him. "I just locked myself out."

He blew out a breath of frustration before disappearing under the stairs. I heard a clang as he tossed something on the ground, and when he reappeared, his face was pale. "Very carefully," he said in a quiet voice, "I want you to put your phone in your pocket." I did as he instructed, sweat popping out on my face even though it was still quite cool out, as clouds covered the sky. "Okay," he said. "I think you can fit under the bottom rung of the rail. Slowly, I want you to sit down and scooch under it. I'll be right here to grab you."

"Stetson," I whispered, almost crying even as I obeyed him, "what's going on?"

"I'll tell you in a second," he promised, and I felt his hands grasp my ankles as I bent my knees over the edge of the landing. I bit my lip, a sliver going into my palm as I eased the rest of my hips under the rung, grasping the railing with all my strength as I laid down on my back.

At the most, it was about a ten-foot drop from the landing to the ground, and with Stetson helping me down, the likelihood of breaking something wasn't even possible. Fear over what he wasn't telling me rendered me almost frantic, and by the time his hands had slid up my calves as he coaxed me down with soothing words, I was crying. The underside of the rail pressed down hard on my chest as I squirmed under it, though it was better than sliding down on my belly and getting a face full of splinters.

When his hands met my waist, holding my belt firmly, I gripped the railing tightly, extending myself down a hair farther. It was all Stetson needed though, for he said, wrapping his arms around my hips, "I've got you now. You can let go."

Trusting him despite my fear, I did, almost falling when my feet met the ground, and if it wasn't for Stetson's strong arms around me, I'm sure I would have crumpled into a ball on the dirt.

"What's going on?" I asked, our noses less than an inch apart, and when his eyes only darkened as he jerked his chin in the direction behind me, my stomach sank.

Pulling away from him, I turned and promptly covered my mouth with both hands to hold in a sob of fear and relief. A pitchfork was laying on the ground next to the landing, a good twelve inches of the wooden handle covered in dirt, its thick prongs menacingly reflecting the early morning light.

"Oh, my word," I breathed, and taking a step back, I bumped into Stetson.

"No kidding," he said. "If you look up by the top stringer, you can see it's been almost sawed through. If you'd have put your weight on the top step, the whole thing would have given out and ..." I felt his chin brush the top of my head as he looked down at me. "Well, we wouldn't be having this conversation."

"I think I'm gonna throw up," I muttered, and when I turned to the side, bending at the waist, Stetson supported me as I vomited. Sweat dripped down my back and chest as I heaved, realizing just how close, once again, I'd come to being killed. Looking back at the pitchfork, I wiped my mouth with the hem of my shirt. The first time someone had tried to murder me, it had been in a rather painless way. This time, though, if Stetson hadn't have appeared when he did, I would have suffered a horrible death, one that had taken a lot of thought and hard work to set up.

Once Stetson had seated me on the bottom landing and supplied me with a piece of mint gum, turning me so that I couldn't see the pitchfork, my thoughts darted back to my mirror coming off the wall, and I closed my eyes, sending up a thankful prayer. Clearly, Someone was looking out for me, and I knew that was the only reason I was still alive. First the mirror, then my keys, delaying me just long enough so that Stetson would be able to save me, and I bowed my head until my forehead brushed against the knees I'd drawn up against my chest.

Stetson was a few feet away, though he kept me in his sight as he paced, having a terse conversation with Blaze, and I kept hearing the phrases 'shouldn't be too much longer at this point,' and 'pre-mediated murder.' I stared hard at the ground, shivering, and the happiness that had enveloped me the day before was gone, leaving me scared and wondering how much longer I would have to live this nightmare. It was bad enough to know there was a killer on the loose, but to know that you're their next target? It's a sickening feeling, a dark feeling, and by the time Stetson ended his phone call, I was rocking back and forth, my eyes burning with tears.

He came and stood in front of me, boots dusty, jeans sporting a small stain on the left cuff, and I looked up at him. "I guess I'm not working today, huh?"

He offered me a hand and pulled me to my feet, and I smelled gun oil on him. My head pounded from the white light pouring down on us from the cloudy sky.

"Actually, no, you're still going to work, because that's probably going to be the safest place for you. Terri just got back in town, and she will be acting as your bodyguard, something no one will notice since she already works for you."

We walked toward my back door, and the five steps it took us to get there seemed like a mile. Stetson continued his instructions, and my skin pinpricked. "You are to go nowhere without Terri, not even the restroom, and once we get your stairs repaired, Blaze is going to check out your flat. From this point on, you're in what is known as protective custody. We're at a point now where the killer is getting desperate, and this setup took quite a bit of thought."

Resting my hand on the metal doorknob, I stared at my feet as I listened to Brey sing in the kitchen while cooking. "Obviously, with Cody in jail, this wasn't him. Can Blaze hold him much longer on empty charges?"

Stetson rested his hand on my mine, and when I finally met his eyes, swallowing the gum, he gave me a grim smile. "Cody is in protective custody, too. We have to assume that since he was framed, if we were to let him out, he would be a target for the killer."

"Like me," I whispered, and when Stetson only nodded, I let out a deep breath. "I don't think I can take much more of this, Stetson."

He motioned for me to open the door, dropping his hand. "The good thing is, you don't have to. Blaze and I are pretty close to catching the killer, we just need you hold out a little bit longer."

A blast of cold air and the smell of frying bacon hit me in the face when I opened the door. "Then I guess I won't have a nervous breakdown yet." Looking into the kitchen, I saw that Terri had already arrived and was covertly securing the place while Brey ran back and forth into the dining area with hot plates, occasionally pausing to flip pancakes.

After giving Stetson a hug, I stepped inside. "I usually don't have to thank people for tasks as big as saving my life, and I wish there was something I could do to repay you, but—"

Stetson cut me off, raising his hand. "Saying thanks is more than enough," he said, resting his other hand on his hip. "I didn't join the force to be thanked or repaid." He looked past me and jerked his chin at Terri. "Keep her safe," he said, "and don't hesitate to call for backup. I'll be at the station training the newbie. We're only a block away, and I'd rather you were overly cautious."

Heading toward the stove, I pulled on the apron Brey tossed at me as she came back in, Terri sending Stetson a nod. "Will do," she said, and for the first time, I saw her as not just a dispatcher, not just a gossipy hen who mothered everyone she could, but as the cop she was. I immediately relaxed, knowing that as long as I was with her, I would be safe.

After a few more warnings, Stetson left. I was almost at a loss as to what to do, until Terri slapped a box of butter in my hands and said, "Those biscuits ain't gonna make themselves. Get a move on."

Brey let out a laugh, and the headache that had begun to throb behind my eyes eased, the heavy roar of hungry customers a soothing sound. The day after the Fourth is always super busy, as the tourists want to get in a good breakfast before hitting the road home, and most of the storeowners are too tired from tending their stands the day before to want to make their own food.

I sent Misty and Mabel a text to let them know what was going on, and Misty promised to be out later, most of her morning would be taken up by a three-hour session with some celebrities. Mabel offered to come out in the afternoon after she squared some things away with a client for the insurance company, promising to hurry.

As I measured out sugar and salt, Terri sidled up next to me, quickly and powerfully hand-whisking a batch of brownie mix that would be used as a filling for a new cupcake we'd started making the month before. "Brey's clean, if you were curious," she said from the corner of her mouth. I gave her bowl an appreciative sniff as she gave it one last stir. The smell of chocolate teased my stomach, though it'd been less than fifteen minutes since I'd thrown up.

"Oh?" I raised an eyebrow as I started rolling out the thick biscuit dough. "Even though I'd never in a million years look in her direction, how do you know that?"

Terri set the bowl down and reached into a drawer for a frosting bottle. "Because she got home to a flooded apartment. Her water line broke, so after she got everything turned off and cleaned up, she spent the night with Misty because her asthma started acting up from the humidity, and you know that girl doesn't have AC."

"New order," Brey called. "Mountain Man Prize, extra pig, no frills, and double the cheese." I moved to the fridge and grabbed a pack of bacon, laying strips on the griddle. The request belonged to Jeff, the only person to ever order the dish with no frills—onions and peppers—and demand more cheese. The dish already came smothered in white cheese sauce and topped with shredded cheddar, but apparently, that wasn't enough for the doctor. Before I knew it, I had been at work for almost four hours, the day going by so fast I could barely keep up.

I'd mostly been able to put the morning behind me and was laughing and joking with Brey when Mitch and Kasey entered the kitchen. They'd called earlier, saying they had something they wanted to show me.

"What's up, guys?" I asked, leaning against the counter, the flow of customers finally starting to slow down. "Do you want anything to eat?"

"Toast sounds good," Mitch said. "And maybe some orange juice?" Kasey wanted an omelet, and once I had everything prepared, I joined them at the folding table we'd left set up in a corner, learning to work around it. Brey and Kasey were sending each other shy smiles, and when I looked at my waitress, she was bright red.

"You're leaving soon, right?" Terri said, cracking eggs on the griddle for a platter that had just been ordered. "Tomorrow?"

Mitch nodded, taking a bite of his toast. "Yeah. We gotta be back in L.A. for a meeting on Friday, otherwise we'd stay a bit longer." He grinned at his food. "Good toast, by the way."

"But that's not why we came over," Kasey said, pushing his empty plate away. "Not to just beg food off you. We actually caught something on video yesterday you should see." He pulled a laptop out of the bag he always had slung over one shoulder and opened it, pressing the power button. "I think you need to rethink your suspect list."

Glancing at Terri, I waited for her to nod before moving. Sitting down next to Kasey, I filled him and Mitch in on what had happened the night before and my near-death experience that morning. They stared at me, Kasey's hands frozen above his keyboard, Mitch shaking his head. "I'm not even surprised anymore," he said. "If you didn't have bad luck, you wouldn't have any."

"I have God," I told him quietly. "And right now, I believe He's the only reason I'm alive."

"Maybe this'll help," Kasey said, turning the laptop toward me. He hit play and I watched as he and Mitch vlogged their day, and he hit another button, skipping forward until the video was showing the footage of Cody's ranch. I watched in silence, Terri standing by my shoulder while Brey took care of customers. "I don't see anything unusual," I told Kasey. "What am I looking for?"

"We set up a time lapse camera around three, facing the plains," Mitch explained. "And we got a good hour of footage of that before someone bumped the camera." I watched the screen, nodding when the camera suddenly tilted, then was righted with a whispered apology. When the scene came back in focus, it was a different direction, giving a close up of a barn. Another minute passed before Cody appeared, walking toward his main barn, which was out of sight of everyone on the ranch, as it was on the other side of the house, and a few seconds after that, a familiar platinum blond showed up, hurrying toward him.

They were only about six feet from the camera, but obviously they'd thought it was off when the lens had pulled in. When they started talking, I realized the sound was gone. "No mic," Kasey said. "No need to use one in a video like this. We just tape classy music over it anyway."

Nodding, I focused on the woman I'd watched leave town the morning before, wondering why she'd lied, and I almost choked on my sip of water when she and Cody suddenly engaged in a passionate kiss, though it lasted less than five seconds. Behind me, I heard Terri muttering to herself. Cody pushed Lacey away, shaking his head even as she clearly yelled at him. He raised his hands, palms outward, his face twisted, but even without sound I knew they were arguing over how he was always leading Lacey on.

Lacey started crying and walked toward the camera, and there was no missing the anger on her face as she wiped at her eyes, smearing her mascara. Cody stared after her, a helpless look on his handsome features, and I knew what Kasey meant about rethinking our suspect list. This video could incriminate Lacey of planting the drugs on Cody's property, since their fight was most likely over Cody still holding out for Vicki. Plus, it caught Lacey right in the middle of a lie, and a big one at that. At this point, Blaze could possibly have enough evidence to arrest her. How she could have planted the drugs in that short of time was beyond me, but, then again, someone had tried to kill me with a pitchfork, so I wasn't ruling anything out.

I even meant to say so, but the words that popped out of my mouth were the exact opposite. "There is no way on this green earth Lacey murdered Vicki and tried to murder me. There just isn't."

"Sometimes people do things we can't comprehend," Mitch said softly, but I shook my head.

"That's true, but not in this case. I know Lacey. She didn't kill Vicki, and she didn't frame Cody."

Mitch opened his mouth, a sharp gleam in his eyes, but before we could argue further, Terri cut us off, leaning over my shoulder to tap the table. "Maybe, instead of bickering about it, you should ask her to come over and confront her. I think Aubrey's right about Lacey being innocent in connection with the murder, but we do need to find out why she lied to everyone."

"Could be what Mitch is saying," Brey said, carefully drizzling peanut butter sauce over a stack of pancakes. "Or maybe the reason she lied is because she was ending things with Cody for good, and she didn't want anyone to know about it. She's probably embarrassed and hurt."

Looking around at everyone, I made the decision. "Okay, I'll call her and ask her to come over. We were talking on the phone this morning about Cody's arrest, which she's pretty upset about, I might add, so she probably sees me as an ally right now." I checked the clock. "Mabel will be here in less than two hours, but I think we might have better luck talking to Lacey without her."

"Good idea," Terri said. "They're both overly dramatic, so it wouldn't do well to put them together." She paused. "We should probably let Blaze handle this, but I think we'll have a better chance of Lacey telling the truth than he will."

"It's settled then," I said, standing. Leaving everyone in the kitchen, I moved into the hallway and grabbed the phone, dialing Lacey's number. She answered on the first ring and sounded almost relieved to accept my invitation to come over for a late lunch.

"I'd love to," she said wearily. "I know what you told me this morning, but it's taking everything I've got to not march over to that station and post bail. I've got enough in the bank to do it, too." She let out a sigh. "Just let me finish up unboxing this order of nail polish and I'll be right over."

I told her to take her time, hung up, and found four pairs of eyes staring at me as I rounded the corner, Brey stirring cake batter while looking over her shoulder. "She's coming over," I said, "and I think it'd be best if you two weren't here." I pointed at Mitch and Kasey. "She won't feel comfortable talking about it in front of two guys, but if it's just us girls, she should open up."

"On that note, then," Kasey said, pushing his chair away from the table, "I'm outta here. All you gotta say is 'girl talk,' and I'll leave." He gave me a quick tutorial on using the laptop, and after packing them a small paper sack of bakery goodies, I sent them on their way, Kasey promising to call Brey later. The young woman blushed and turned back to her task, but not before I saw the smile that spread across her face.

Looking at Terri, I frowned. "If things turn bad, can you handle it?"

She nodded and touched the small of her back, and for the first time, I noticed she was wearing a baggy shirt that hid her strong frame. "I'm armed and willing to do what I have to. Though I doubt Lacey will get violent even if she is the killer, I'll still let Blaze know what's going on so he can be kept in the loop." She raised her shirt to show me the small handgun strapped to the inside of her belt and neatly hidden against the hollow of her back, and I swallowed hard, meeting her harsh gaze. If things weren't already to the point of leaving me in cold sweats, I'd be quaking at the situation I was in, but after a murder and two attempts on my own life, I was no longer able capable of being shocked. All I could feel was a calm assuredness that this ordeal was almost over, but whether or not I came out of it alive was yet to be seen.

"I LIED because I knew he was going to reject me," Lacey bawled into my shoulder as we sat side by side at the folding table. "But I had to try!"

Her sobs almost drowned out the hum of the dishwasher as it entered its rinse cycle, and thankfully, the only person in the dining area was Jeanine, an older woman who came into town every other week. She spent five or six hours at a table reading a book and enjoying several pots of coffee and more than a few Danishes. I say thankfully, because she was going on eighty-one and is hard of hearing, so we had no need to worry about her overhearing anything.

Terri's eyes met mine as she quietly rolled out a pie crust on the counter next to us. They were serious, yet sympathetic, as were Brey's as she carefully frosted carrot cookies. "Guilty?" I mouthed to Terri over Lacey's head as the beautician cried, but Terri shook her head, and I agreed.

After sweetening Lacey up with a coffee and some mini strawberry glazed donuts, I'd been straight and to the point. Turning on the laptop, I'd confronted her with the condemning video, only to have her break down and spill the truth about how she'd been carrying the torch for Cody for years, only for the rancher to throw it back in her face time and time again.

"If that had been all," she'd sobbed into her hands, her mascara blackened tears dripping between her fingers and to the tabletop below, "I could have moved on, but he keeps stringing me along. Even I know he's been playing me. But sometimes he texts me, sometimes he calls me, says he misses me, and even when he's saying no, he's kissing me. I don't know what to feel."

"Yesterday was your final effort, wasn't it?" Terri said as she draped the crust into a glass pie pan and started pricking it with a fork. "You're done with him, now, aren't you?"

Pulling away from me, Lacey scrubbed her hands over her eyes, her eyeshadow and mascara now smudged memories of the masterpieces they had been that morning. "Yes," she sniffed, and I breathed in a deep breath of fresh air tinged with the tart scent of the chopped cherries Brey was adding into a bowl, relieved to not be inhaling Lacey's hair anymore. "Yes," she said again, staring at the table. "I had a few weak moments this morning, wanting to bail him out, but Aubrey kept me sane."

"Love is like that," Brey commented, washing her hands, and I shivered as the AC kicked in. "Makes you do the dumbest things."

"I've never loved someone like I love him," Lacey admitted. "I feel like I'm going crazy." She looked at me and twisted her lips into a wistful smile, her loose hair flowing down her back, green blouse shimmering in the light as she sighed. "But not all love is returned. I need to let him go."

"And that's what you did yesterday?" Terri asked, giving the pie-making task to Brey as she texted Blaze, her hands less than a foot away from the back of Lacey's head.

Lacey nodded. "Yes. Then I went home." She tapped a sandaled foot on the floor. "Look, I know you guys are trying to figure out if I planted the drugs in his barn, not that I blame you, but I can prove that I didn't." She pulled her phone from her pocket. "I facetimed my mom last night. She can vouch for that, and so can the location of my phone if Terri wants to look it up with my provider."

Clucking her tongue, Terri said, "No, that's not necessary. But, Lacey, all things case-related aside, because I believe you're telling us the truth, you need to get over Cody. No one is worth the pain he's been putting you through."

"Amen to that, sister," Brey muttered, dumping the pie mixture into the pan that held the crust.

"I've been there, you know," I told Lacey. After handing her a napkin, I recounted my own sorry love story, which had seemed like a fairy tale, until I was left at the altar.

"I thought I could never love again," I said, my words frank, my tone sad, "but then, well, after living here for a while, I realized that wasn't true, and—" my words were cut off when Terri's phone started chirping, and holding up a finger, she answered it.

"Terri," she barked into it, and after a few "Hmms," and a couple "I sees," she hung up and heaved a sighed before looking at me. "That was Blaze," she said. "He just got off the phone with Mabel and is on his way to pick her up right now. She was coming into the shop but couldn't get her car to stop at the stop sign." Terri met my gaze. "Aubrey, someone tried to kill her."

Amidst Brey's gasp and Lacey's muted shriek, I said, "Let me guess, someone cut her brake lines."

Terri nodded. "Yep. Had she not braked for a deer at the end of her road, she wouldn't have found out until she merged onto the highway. That could have been a very different phone call."

"God's been watching out for us," Brey said, and I nodded, having told her and Terri about my strange experience with the bathroom mirror that morning.

"What's this mean for us, then?" Lacey rubbed her chin, gray eyes wide.

Terri glared at the table for a long moment before answering. "It means the killer is getting reckless. They aren't focusing on the same person anymore." Here, she looked at me. "They're targeting multiple people, and obviously, they don't care how they have to do it, or how messy the outcome might be."

"We're in trouble, aren't we?" I whispered.

Terri nodded. "That's what it looks like."

Brey gave me a remorseful look. "Guess that means we won't make 'Town of the Year' this fall, will we?"

"I HAVE A BUSINESS TO RUN. Nowhere in the words 'protective custody' does it allow me to do that. So, no, I'm not moving to your ranch." I said the words slowly and clearly, as if Blaze was hard of hearing. Yelling them hadn't worked, and I wasn't about to beg.

"You don't get a choice in this," he replied, staring down at me as Terri and Brey tried to look busy flipping pancakes, Lacey having left only moments before. "There is no yes or no from you. I'm telling you what you're going to do, and that's it. You do it."

"What am I, a pup in training?" I retorted.

Blaze laughed. "If you are, you're the cutest one yet," he chuckled. Just as quickly, he sobered, touching my shoulder as we stood in the corner by the sink. "But like it or not, you, Misty, and Mabel are going to my ranch. It's not like you'll be alone, and I promise, it'll only be for a few days." He had just ended the call to Misty, letting her know what was going on, and had sent Stetson over to guard her as she finished up her class. If Mabel and I were targets, it was a pretty good assumption that she was as well.

"What about my clothes?" I asked. "If I can't get in my apartment, how am I supposed to pack?"

"I'm pretty sure Misty has everything you'd need," came the reply. "Now stop complaining. This is happening, whether you like it or not."

"Come on, Aubrey," Mabel said as she came out of the restroom, drying her hands. "It'll be fun. We can redecorate his house, mess up his kitchen, and eat his food."

I eyed my friend. Despite the fact it'd been less than an hour since she'd found out her brakes had been tampered with, which could have ended very badly, she looked bright and peppy. Letting out a groan, I agreed.

"Fine," I snapped. "But I won't be happy about it."

BLAZE HAD NEVER STRUCK me as a guy who would decorate his house in such a welcoming way, but I felt at home almost as soon as I walked in the door. One hand clutching my purse, the other holding a container of goodies, I followed Blaze as he shown us around, only tripping once over a pile of rope he'd left in the middle of the foyer. He promised to give me a tour of the ranch itself the next morning, before he left for the station, and amid the muted giggles of my two companions, I agreed to the plan of an early breakfast by the pond in the south pasture.

Of the four spare bedrooms, I'd chosen the one with a cowhide hanging on one wall and a weathered saddle on the other, the pale green blanket that covered the bed begging me to curl up in it with a good book snagged from the bookcase that leaned against a wall.

Gazing out the dining room window later that day, my shoulders relaxed as I watched the golden fingers of the sinking sun caress the green grass and bright flowers that grew along the fence. Even though Blaze owned about as much land as Cody, he didn't have much livestock, his barn housing only a handful of cows and three horses. He'd lived in Flamingo Springs for less than a year and hadn't had the time nor the funds to fully get the ranch going, because police work took most of his time. Because of that, he was the only one who lived on the several acres of land that had been named "Martin Pastures," and he had no need for hired help yet. As Misty dug out a game of Monopoly from the closet behind us, I could see why he spent so much time at the station.

Blaze had no one to go home to at night, no family and no pets, unless you counted the barnyard animals. Even Cody had someone to talk to, because three of his ranch hands lived in the house with him, acting as roommates and brothers, but Blaze didn't have any of that. In fact, besides Stetson, I was beginning to wonder if perhaps he didn't have any friends at all. My heart ached a little bit to think of him rattling around inside his big house, no one to talk to, no one to be with. It wasn't until Mabel slapped the board game down on the table in front of me that I realized I'd been woolgathering and had completely missed the conversation she and Misty had been having.

"Who wants to be the banker?" Mabel asked, but I only shook my head while Misty decided which player token she wanted. The chicken potpie we'd bought from Jesse heated in the oven, and its smell wafted through the air. Mabel finally grabbed the bag of money and dealt out the opening hand of cash to each player.

We hadn't talked much about the attempts on our lives, mainly, I think, because it creeped us out too much. What little Mabel had said left me in chills, and she'd almost lost it when Blaze had told her what had happened to me that morning. Misty whispered prayers under her breath, her clear eyes clouded with worry, and I knew she was wondering if she was next.

"This truly is a beautiful home," she now said as she rolled the dice and bought a property. "I can only imagine what it will look like in five or six years when he's built his stock and has a few ranch hands working for him."

"The man has an eye for color, that's for sure," I said, glaring at her, daring her to buy the railroad tracks she'd landed on with her double roll. "I love the green he painted it in here."

"Warm," Mabel interjected, handing Misty the railroad card along with some change while Misty smirked. "I can't think of any other way to describe it here, except as warm."

"I agree," Misty said, handing me the dice. "This is a home to raise children in, a place to have friends over often. I imagine that at Christmas, this could be really beautiful if it's all decked out with lights and garland." She gestured toward the living room, which the dining area opened into. Most of Blaze's house was set in an open-style concept.

Mabel and I nodded at that one, and we continued playing. Misty filed for bankruptcy twice but Mabel either forgave her debts or loaned her money from the bank— we have our own rules— and we tossed around ideas of how we'd decorate Blaze's house for the holidays.

But while my friends talked about all the grand things they'd do with the living room, the size of tree they'd bring in, all I could envision was a fire roaring away in the stone fireplace with framed family photos atop the mantle's ledge, a live pine tree draped in bright lights and crowded with presents standing in the corner. I could almost hear Amy Grant singing Christmas hymns, and if I looked hard enough, I could see the shadows of Blaze and his family moving about, children chasing a puppy around the room while he placed a kiss on his wife's cheek as she carried in a plate of homemade scones. Scones that looked a lot like the ones I ma—Nope. No way was I going there.

"You owe me nine thousand dollars," I told Misty sternly after she landed on Boardwalk. As she sorted through her pitiful amount of money and turned over her property cards to see how much they were worth, I gave myself an even more stern talking too, refusing to allow myself to daydream any longer.

But even after we'd finished our game, eaten supper, and cleaned the kitchen, I couldn't shake the almost bittersweet feeling that had come over me. When we headed for bed, my nose twitching at the lavender scent that rose from the pajamas Misty had loaned me, I found myself humming a Christmas song under my breath.

13

The sound of my alarm going off woke me up early the next morning, and I groaned. Morning comes to a ranch much earlier than it does to a bakery. I curled up under the thick comforter, enjoying the coolness of the room as cold air blasted out of the vent in the floor, debating how much I wanted to go on that ride with Blaze.

My lips curled up as I thought of the handsome sheriff, and though I'd never tell anyone, it hadn't been until he'd finally gotten home the night before that I'd been able to fall asleep. I'd listened to the sounds of him moving around the kitchen, putting together his late supper, before making his way down the hallway to the master bedroom, softly whistling a jaunty tune.

Since I could smell coffee in the air, it was obvious he was already up. When I plodded out into the kitchen half an hour later, showered, dressed, and feeling a bit more awake, he was seated at the table in the kitchen, sipping coffee and biting into one of the muffins I'd brought over.

Looking up at me as he raised the mug to his lips, he cocked an eyebrow, and I glanced at what he'd been reading. It looked

like he was working his way through the book of Judges, a
rather hefty book of the Bible. Once he'd swallowed and set the
mug back down, he sent me a grin. "Sleep well?" he asked playfully, and when I only stared at him, he laughed.

"I could hear you snoring when I came past your room this
morning," he said. "You must have been worn out."

"Sleep hasn't been my friend lately," I admitted, knowing
how badly I snored when I was exhausted. I poured myself a
mug of coffee from the old-fashioned pot that sat on the
stovetop and placed a muffin on a saucer from the stack he'd
set out. Since it was barely five, Misty and Mabel were still
asleep. I sat down next to him, stretching my legs out under the
table.

Glancing at Blaze, I found him staring at me. The pale blue
shirt he wore highlighted his tan. I quickly looked away and
stared into my coffee cup, but I couldn't deny how right everything seemed, how perfect and natural it seemed to be having
coffee with him while a Bible sat between us, pale light pouring
through the windows.

Blaze spoke, startling me. "Life has a way of surprising you,
doesn't it?" he said, and his odd tone had me looking at him
again. His grin was gone, replaced by a type of seriousness I'd
not seen him display before, and without giving me time to
answer him, he went on. "One moment you think you know
how your life is going to go, and just like," he snapped his
fingers, the sound loud in the silence that surrounded us,
"everything changes."

When I nodded, he reached over and placed his warm hand
on top of mine where it lay on the table. "Thing is," he said,
"sometimes when life changes, it's for the very best, and it's
more beautiful than you could have ever imagined."

Getting a good grasp on what he was saying, I swallowed
hard, and when his gaze dropped to my lips, my mind went
back to the first kiss we'd shared. My face flushed as I remem-

bered it in great detail. I shoved my chair back, squeaking the feet on the wood floor. "Ready to show me that pond?" I asked, my voice a bit higher than normal, but when Blaze only grinned and joined me, placing his dishes in the sink after closing the Bible, I knew I hadn't fooled him in the slightest.

"Sure," he said. "Let me get you one of my hats." He led me to the front door where he plopped a hat on my head and grabbed his own, then took me out to the barn behind the house. He introduced me to the six cows and the three horses, and after being a gentleman and saddling my mare—a gentle thing he'd named April—he handed me the reins while he saddled his own horse, a strong stallion named Fury. The four-year-old had streaks of white running through his black coat, a strong contrast to April's blond coloring, but he, too, displayed a gentle side, resting his head on Blaze's shoulder.

"You do know how to mount and ride, right?" Blaze asked, once we'd led our steeds into the yard, and I gave him a haughty look and proceeded to clumsily crawl on top of April. It'd been a few months since I'd ridden a horse, and I could count on one hand the times I'd done it, but no way was I going to tell him that.

"Yes," I told him smartly after gaining my balance. He was wise enough to not laugh, swinging up on Fury. Nudging our mounts, we set off, and before long, the house was out of sight.

To say that Blaze's ranch is breathtaking would be an understatement. As we rode, he pointed out various landmarks and oddities, showing me groups of blossoming flowers and the trees his favorite birds nested in. The sun hadn't broken the horizon, but it was already bright out, the pale blue sky clear with hints of gold in the east. The air was still cool, and I was a bit chilled despite wearing a flannel shirt and jeans.

When we reached the pond, we dismounted, letting the horses wander off a few yards. We were next to a birch tree, its long branches covered in bright green leaves that housed a few squirrels and barn swallows. After we'd settled down on the quilt Blaze pulled from one of my saddlebags, we sipped coffee and nibbled on apples from the small knapsack he'd carried with him. I stared out over the pond, admiring the ducks that were lazily swimming around it. The soft rustle of the wind blew through the grass and provided a soothing background noise.

"You have a beautiful place," I finally told Blaze, forcing myself to speak past the lump of shyness that had suddenly clogged my throat. I drew in a deep breath of fresh air tinged with the sweet scent of grass, meeting his eyes as I took my hat off.

"Thanks," he said with a smile. "Took me almost ten years of saving every penny I got my hands on, but it's definitely worth it." He gestured at the flat plains that stretched out in front of us, telling me of his plans to one day build his herd. If I squinted, raising my hand to shield my eyes against the sun that had finally appeared, I could make out the southern fence he'd been building in his spare time. The more he talked, the more I could see what he envisioned for his land, and it was an attractive sight.

"You like it out here, don't you?" he asked, moving closer to me, his shoulder brushing mine as we leaned back against the tree.

Fiddling with the buttons of my shirt, I undid the top two before answering. The air grew warmer as the sun slowly rose. "I do," I admitted. "When I first moved here, I wasn't so sure how much I would like the country, being a city girl and all, but it didn't take me long to fall in love with it." My words caught a bit as Blaze slid his hand over mine. "I love Texas."

"What about here?" he pushed. "Out here on a ranch?"

Looking at him, I knew exactly what he was asking. He stared into my eyes for a long moment, then nodded, as if he'd found the answer in them without me having to say one word.

When he leaned down, his broad shoulder pressing mine back against the tree, I reached up and knocked his hat off his head.

"Why do you always do that?" he asked, sounding slightly aggravated. I heard undertones of laughter in his voice, his dimples deepening as he struggled to hold back a smile.

"Because," I said, tugging on a thick strand of smooth hair. "I like touching your hair." I pulled on the strand a bit harder. "Now, are you gonna kiss me or what?"

"You're a spitfire, Aubrey," Blaze whispered, letting me pull his head down. I closed my eyes as his breath hit my cheek, and the last thing I heard him say before our lips met was, "Good thing I like that."

WE STAYED under the tree for the next hour, discussing everything from politics to Bible passages. When we mounted up and started back toward the house, Blaze looked over at me, one hand loosely holding his reins, the other resting on his thigh. "You never talk about yourself," he said.

Shrugging, I reached forward to pat April's glossy neck. She rewarded me by tossing her head back, asking for more, and I scratched between her ears, having quickly bonded with the sweet-natured horse. "Not much to tell," I said, starting to sweat a little under the warm sun.

"Everyone has something to tell," Blaze told me. "You've heard my story, how I wanted to live in small town. So, what's yours'?"

Fiddling with the reins for a moment, my mind went back to the reason I'd left New York. "I grew up in Manhattan," I said, "and went to culinary school right after graduation. I started dating this guy in eleventh grade, and we were together for years, even when he went to Germany to study for a year while I stayed behind and got my degree in all things kitchen related." I drew in a deep breath. "He proposed when we were twenty-four, and I'd just turned twenty-five when it was time to walk down the aisle, only he wasn't there to meet me."

Glancing at Blaze who was looking straight ahead, I wiped an errant tear out of my eye. Though I'd long moved on from any feelings for my ex-fiancé, his actions still stung. "What happened?" he asked, and I could hear the sympathy in his voice.

"He hooked up with my maid of honor, who was dating the best man. The day that was supposed to be the start to my happily ever after turned out to be, well ..." I paused, thinking. "I could say it was the worst day of my life, but was it really? I mean, it's better that it happened before I said 'I do' instead of after. But it was still a pretty hard pill to swallow."

Chest lifting with a sigh, I stared at the house as it slowly took shape in front of us and recounted the crazy reception I'd had, which had included smashing my ex's cake figurine with a hammer. "I still have the pictures somewhere," I said, "of me smashing that cake in his face when he decided it would be a good idea to show up." I chuckled.

Blaze listened intently, now watching me, his eyes hooded in the shadow of his hat.

"After that, I decided I couldn't bear to stay in New York anymore, couldn't live with the memories, so I called the airport and asked the booking agent to give me a one-way ticket to the prettiest sounding place she could find, as long as she kept it in my price rang. She said she knew the perfect place, a small town called Flamingo Springs that she used to visit as a child. So, I packed everything up and came down here. I fell in love with it and knew from the moment I arrived, this is where I was meant to be."

We arrived in the barnyard, and Blaze slid off Fury, then came around to help me to the ground "Do you regret it?" he asked softly, looking down at me, hands resting on my hips.

I tilted the brim of my slightly too big hat back so that I could look up at him. "I used to," I told him honestly, placing my hands on his forearms, feeling them tense as I did so. I met his eyes, hearing Mabel's cackle echo through the air as she yelled something at Misty, their voices drifting through the open kitchen window. For some reason, the sound gave me the courage to speak the words I was holding back. "But not anymore."

"Y'all want bacon?" Misty yelled out at us just then, breaking the rather intimate moment. Blaze grinned. "Who could refuse bacon?" he chuckled before yelling, "Sure." Looking back at me, he pressed a kiss to my forehead. "I was in the same boat," he whispered. Pulling back, he pinned me down with a serious look. "But not anymore."

Something shifted between us as I nodded, but before I could further examine what that something could be, Blaze's phone chirped, and he pulled away, checking it. "I need to get to the station," he said. "Just save me some bacon, okay?"

Teasingly arguing with him about eating it all, I helped him put Fury and April out to graze in the pasture behind the barn. As I stood on the large porch a few minutes later, watching dust kick up behind his truck as he drove toward town, my shoulders heaved with another sigh.

Checking my phone, I saw it was well past eight, and I dialed the bakery's number as I headed toward the house, smiling when Terri answered. "I know," she said. "Today's Tuesday, so that means upside down pineapple pancakes and cinnamon swirl pancakes for the special. Brey just pulled her third pan of cupcakes from the oven, and we've got the lavender lemonade steeping in the fridge."

"I trust you completely," I said drily when she paused to take a breath. "Maybe I should just leave the shop to you two and spend my days writing a book or something." I frowned when I heard a distinctly male voice asking how to make peanut butter sauce. "Is that Mitch?" I asked suspiciously.

The words came out louder than I'd meant them to, because I heard him yell "Hello, Aubrey!" before Terri answered. "Yes," she said, sounding a bit sheepish. "We're a bit overrun today, but Mitch and Kasey were more than happy to help us out when Brey explained everything to them. Since their meeting got moved out a week, they've decided to stay a bit longer. They actually make pretty good waiters, and Kasey has been flipping pancakes like he was born holding a spatula."

"Maybe I should come in," I said, stepping inside the house and kicking my sneakers off. "Let me change, and I'll be right out."

"No, you won't," Terri said firmly. "We have everything under control, and besides that, you're in hiding. You can't leave."

"And where am I?" I asked, a bit confused at her odd way of wording things.

"Well," she said. "Oh, hold up a sec, honey, Mitch needs help." She put the phone down and I heard her giving Mitch muted instructions on how to fix a muffin platter. At this point, I was in the kitchen. Misty danced around setting the table with black and blue plates. Mabel worked on juicing the basket of oranges Blaze had by the toaster, face turning red as she worked the hand-powered juicer.

Terri came back. "I know there weren't a lot of details discussed yesterday, but after a lot of thought, we decided that it would be best if everyone thinks you, Misty, and Mabel took an unexpected girls' trip to New York. If anybody asks, we're just telling them the stress was getting to you, so you took the week off. So far, only Jeff has asked where you are, and he said if I talked to you to make sure your head is doing okay. I told him you'd seemed fine when I'd driven you to the airport this morning, but that I'd be sure to text you."

"New York," I said, nodding when Mabel held up a glass of juice. "So, does that mean this thing is almost over?"

Terri sighed, and I could hear a knife repeatedly hitting a cutting board in the background. "Can't say for sure," she said, and moved away from the noise, probably going around the corner and standing by the wall phone. "But we think so. We have our eye on someone, and so far, they haven't left town, so anytime now."

Closing my eyes, I sent up a prayer of gratitude that the nightmare my life had become was almost over, and after thanking Terri again for taking my place at the diner, I got off the phone and joined my friends for breakfast.

"Everyone thinks we're in New York," I told them, biting into a strip of bacon.

"Never been there," Mabel said. "I bet it's nice." She sipped her juice. "Lady Liberty today, ladies? Or Central Park?" I grinned at her, and she laughed.

"How was your morning with Blaze?" Misty asked, and when I looked at her, she had a sly grin on her face, eyes puffy from sleep. "Hope I wasn't interrupting anything when I asked about the bacon."

Mabel threw a napkin at her. "Liar."

Misty laughed as I glared at her. "Well, it just seems like a week ago you and Blaze were at each other's throats, and now you're all kissy-kissy. I'm wondering how that's going."

Slathering my second muffin of the day with butter, I met her eyes. "Quite well, actually. Is this where I ask about Mitch?"

"Oooh," Mabel jeered. "Cat fight."

Misty held her hands up. "I surrender," she laughed. "Don't kill me!"

Brandishing my butter knife at her, I grinned. "Don't tempt me."

After we finished breakfast, Mabel scrolled through Facebook and give us bits of gossip. While she and Misty headed off to shower and dress for the day, I putzed around the kitchen. After loading the dishwasher, I looked in the cupboards to see how Blaze stocked his pantry, thinking a sour cream apple pie with a caramel filling would go well with the roast he'd set out to thaw after I'd asked to make dinner as thanks for staying at his place.

After finding the appropriate ingredients for the pie, including frozen apple slices in the freezer, I hunted around for a pie pan. Next, I went after a rolling pin. Finally finding it with the cutting boards, I reached in to grab it. When my hand brushed over the smooth wooden handle, I froze, my body firing danger signals as a chill went through me.

Carefully, I pulled the utensil out and placed it on the granite countertop. Stepping back, I stared at it, remembering the blood pooled around Vicki's head and the blow that had struck me, almost killing me, though I wasn't sure what kind of weapon my attacker had used. I touched my head, which now only bore a tiny bump and a small bruise.

When Misty and Mabel rejoined me, we went into the living room where we played a game of Risk, but no matter how hard I laughed, I couldn't shake the distinct feeling that I was in more danger than I had been the entire week previous. If I wasn't careful, I would end up joining Vicki.

14

Around lunchtime, after I'd popped the pie in the oven, chills running through me the entire time I'd used the rolling pin, we decided to give Blaze's house a good cleaning. Though he kept it neat, we found ourselves fighting boredom and needed something to keep us busy. We tackled the chore with glee, fluffing pillows, dusting windowsills, and singing as loudly as we could, each trying to outdo the other.

"Since none of us can actually afford a vacation to New York," Mabel yelled from the room she was sweeping, "why don't we plan a weekend or something out at the Spa?"

"We could," Misty hollered from her own room where she was washing windows. "Or we could head to Houston."

"How about both?" I bellowed, all of us giggling. "Go to Houston for two days and crash at the Spa for another two? Like a four-day weekend?" I finished wiping down the sink in the bathroom that connected to my room and joined Misty in the hallway as she headed for Mabel's room.

"We should," Mabel said, filling a dustpan with dirt. "After everything we've been through, I think we should take a real vacation and do girly stuff, like dye our hair or get a massage, or go to a candy store."

"Or all of the above," Misty told her. She fluffed her hair, which was hanging loose down her back. "I need a touch up for this mop, and I was thinking about switching to either blue, or dying it back to brown."

"We could get tattoos," Mabel suggested.

I flopped on her bed, enveloped in a blanket of soft gray, the pale blue walls of her room bright and cheery. "Matching ones?" I asked, doubtfully, my skin having never seen a needle, though Misty sported two tattoos, one on the underside of her wrist, the other on her collarbone. "I don't know."

"We could get them on the sides of our feet," Mabel said as Misty joined me on the bed. "But wherever we decide, let's make sure it's a spot that won't hurt too much." She disappeared into the hallway for a moment to put the broom and dustpan away.

Sniffing the quilt I was sprawled on, the scent of fabric softener reminded me of a cheesy commercial. "It's certainly something to think about," I said. "And I'm all for a weekend away from this madness."

Sitting up, I poked Misty as she rolled over onto her back arms crossed behind her head. Mabel now sat in the rocker in the corner. "You think they'll catch whoever is behind this?"

Misty cracked an eye open. "I have no doubt," she said. "I have a feeling this is almost over." She yawned. "I don't know about you guys, but I kinda want a nap."

"Now that you mention it," I said, feeling the effects of the late night, early morning, and busy afternoon, "I want one, too."

"Me three," Mabel agreed.

Misty and I headed for our rooms, leaving Mabel to crash on her bed. The house smelled like the pie that was cooling on the counter, and I'd put the roast in the oven about an hour earlier, wanting it done when Blaze got home at six. As I lay on the bed, I watched the light play through the curtains and cast shadows on the ceiling. Though I'd finally convinced myself I was safe since everyone thought I was thousands of miles away, and the suspect was under watch, I couldn't help but think about how strange everything was. Here I was on a Tuesday afternoon, taking a nap in one of Blaze's spare bedrooms, my two best friends only feet away as we hid from a killer.

In a week's time, my view of almost everyone in town had changed, but the biggest change of all was my feelings for Blaze. I'd gone from wishing he'd go back to where he'd come from to hoping I could have just one more moment with him, feel his lips against mine just one more time. Never in a million years had I thought I could feel that way about him, or anyone, for that matter, and for the first time since I'd been jilted at the altar, something bright and glorious stirred in my chest.

I don't talk much about my almost wedding day, but it left me feeling like I'm not good enough. It made me think I'm messed up and too complicated for someone to love, and no matter what anyone said, people looked at me with pity in their eyes.

Blaze never made me feel that way. Not one time had I thought I wasn't good enough, or that I needed to earn his love. And when this crazy nightmare is over, I could only hope that he would be the one part of it that doesn't go away.

"You're getting bored here, aren't you?" Blaze chuckled in my ear that evening as he leaned past me to put a bowl in the cupboard.

We'd just finished dinner and shooed Mabel and Misty to the living room where they watched the evening news, leaving Blaze and me to clean the kitchen.

Giving the tan cookie dough one last harsh stir with the wooden spoon, I sprinkled the counter with flour. "What makes you say that?" I asked, placing a glob of the dough on the flour.

Blaze laughed, the low sound sending a shiver through me. When he stole a spoonful of dough, I could only stare as his throat worked, watching the way the light played on his tanned skin, his hair messy from the hat that now hung on the hook by the door. He tossed the spoon in the sink. It clanged loudly.

"Really, Aubrey?" he said, stepping closer to me, and I inhaled the smell of his aftershave. "First a pie, then you cleaned my house, and you made a roast dinner complete with mashed potatoes, gravy, and carrots, and now you're making cookies. Yeah, I think you're bored."

"And if I am?" I retorted, digging through the drying rack for the rolling pin I'd placed there earlier after washing my pie-making dishes. "What am I supposed to do, twiddle my thumbs?"

A warm hand splayed across my lower back as Blaze's other arm snaked past me to switch on the kitchen lights. The sun was beginning to set. "I'm not complaining," he said. "Just making an observation."

Turning, I found my forehead less than an inch from his chin, and I looked up. "Did you move the rolling pin?" I asked.

He shook his head, looking down at me. "No. Why, is that important?"

I gestured to the cookies. "Duh."

Moving forward until my back was against the counter, hidden from anyone in the living room, Blaze placed his hands on either side of me, pressing them flat on the countertop. "Aubrey," he said, "considering the fact we were interrupted this morning, I couldn't care less about the rolling pin." His eyes twinkled as he spoke, and for the moment, I gave up on the pursuit of the rolling pin. He left a few minutes later, carrying a container of food for Stetson, bearing a perfect handprint of flour on his back, dark hair streaked with the powdery substance.

Thankfully, Mabel and Misty were too busy watching a sitcom to notice, and after setting the oven on preheat, I rolled out the cookie dough with a plastic glass. The rolling pin was nowhere to be found, though I'd searched for it in all the cupboards and drawers, and even checked the garbage bin. Laughter floated into the kitchen from the TV, mixed with that of my friends, and despite my worry, I hummed under my breath as I baked pan after pan of cookies.

It was well after midnight when I finished, Misty keeping me company as she sat at the kitchen table, reading a book she'd found in the living room on the importance of exercise and nutrition. She'd scoffed at a few of the ideas, agreed with others, and muttered to herself in a heated debate about one of them. But that was to be expected, since her main form of exercise was yoga, and it seemed Blaze stuck to high-intensity workouts.

When I finally placed the last baked good in a plastic container, the third I'd filled to the brim, she headed for bed, stealing a small cookie as she did so. Twenty minutes later, after I started the dishwasher and wiped everything down, I followed suit. I let out a happy sigh as I slid between the sheets, tired but fulfilled. Terri had kept me abreast of the bakery activity through text messages all day. Mitch and Kasey had sent me goofy pictures and videos of their antics in my kitchen, and after spending a few minutes checking Facebook, I plugged my phone into its charger and rolled onto my side.

Like the night before, I struggled to fall asleep, waiting to hear Blaze come home. But when midnight came and went, the time he'd come home the night before, I decided that like it or not, I was going to have to sleep without him in the house. I'd spent the time waiting for him by going over everything I knew about the case, focusing on each and every detail I could think of, but nothing extreme enough to cause real concern stood out to me, and I knew it was time to give it up for a while. Forcing my eyes shut, I pretended I could hear ocean waves crashing against a shore and synced my inhales and exhales to them.

It didn't take long to fall asleep after that, but it wasn't the peaceful slumber I'd experienced the night before. No, this sleep was filled with nightmares. I was hot and sweaty, like I was suffocating. Everything I'd gone through during the last week flashed through my dream, faster and faster, and a theme began to occur, an accusing finger always pointing at the same person, with a perfect explanation.

The person I'd willed my bakery to was also the one who had suddenly refused to share recipes with me and had become almost irate when I asked about the sudden change. When in costume, that person's shoe size was the exact same as that of the print below Lacey's window. And the skid mark in the dirt when she lost her balance on her stilts matched the ones on not only Vicki's kitchen floor, but mine as well.

Donuts, and bagels, and cookies, oh, my! I struggled to wake up, knowing I was asleep, and the realization of who the killer was threatened to send me into a panic attack.

Something splashed onto my cheek, bringing me out from underneath the heavy cover of sleep. I opened my eyes and let out a hoarse gasp, as if I'd been holding my breath for a long time. My eyes focused, and I realized that Mabel was standing over me on a stepstool, a rolling pin held over her head.

"This will only hurt for a moment," she whispered, almost pleadingly. As I stared up at her, the dim light from the lamp in the corner lit up her face, and I saw that she was crying. The wet splash that had woken me up was a tear that had dripped off her quivering chin.

Her arm arched back a bit higher, then came down. Without thinking, I threw my forearm in front of my face, catching what would have been a killing blow to my temple.

The loud crack of wood striking flesh, breaking my arm, and my scream of pain echoed through the house.

"Stop fighting," Mabel shouted, raising the rolling pin again and leaning forward on the stool. Too dazed to fight her off, I could only roll to the side. The wooden utensil hit my shoulder, and the glancing blow sent sparks across my vision.

"Stop it," I screamed. "Mabel, stop!" I tried to move away but was trapped under the blanket. With one arm broken and the shoulder of the opposite side numb with pain, I knew my chances of making it out of my room alive were slim and getting less likely with every blow Mabel landed. The next one grazed my ear and slammed into my pillow.

A loud yell resounded through the house before my door crashed inward, bouncing off the wall. The sight of my best friend, clad in silk pajamas, green clay mask covering her face, pink hair going in every direction as she came to my rescue, was the most beautiful thing I'd ever seen.

"No," Mabel screamed, trying to get in one last whack at me, but Misty was too fast. Before I could even sit up, Mabel was face down on the rug. The rolling pin skittered across the floor and bumped into the wall, while the stepstool teetered on two feet before settling back down. Misty stradled across Mabel's back, twisting her arms up so high I thought she would rip them off Mabel's body.

"Call Blaze," she hollered over Mabel's angry screams. "And get some rope."

Not sure which to do first, since my body was telling me to pass out and throw up at the same time, I hesitated. Misty shouted at me again, directing me. Sliding out of bed, I ran into the foyer where I'd seen a length of rope, trying not to jostle the limp arm I held against my abdomen. I picked it up with my good hand and ran back to my room, gritting my teeth.

Everything was in sharp focus, as if I'd put sunglasses on in the middle of a sunny day, the smell of dinner and cookies still lingering in the air. My room was cast in shadows from the lamp I'd left on when I'd went to bed, and my skin felt like it was about to peel right off my body.

"Get Blaze on the phone," Misty barked as she grabbed the rope from me. Mabel, face buried in the rag rug by my bed, her muted sobs reaching my ears, no longer fought Misty. Stepping around them, I grabbed my phone. Unlocking it, I saw that both Blaze and Stetson had tried to call me numerous times, but because it was set on vibrate, I'd slept right through their attempts. I tapped Blaze's name and held down the green icon. When he picked up a few rings later, I could feel his worry as he spoke.

"I'm on my way," he ground out before I could say a word. "I just figured it out. Tell me you're okay."

I sank down onto the floor, my arm now hanging loosely at my side while Misty secured Mabel. "I'm fine," I managed to get out past the vomit that clogged back of my throat. "We've got her."

"Thank God," he breathed, and I heard him lay on the horn at something in the road. "I'm almost there," he said. "Hang on, okay?"

"Blaze," I croaked out, starting to slump forward as the full pain of my broken arm finally reached me. "Blaze, I need you."

His panicked voice faded as I toppled over and landed on the rug next to Mabel. And then, there was blissful darkness.

15

Blaze's green eyes were the first thing I saw when I came to a while later. "This is the second time I've woken up to this. I could get used to it."

The worry left his face as he laughed. I blinked, only then realizing what I'd just said. "No," he chuckled, refusing to allow me to cover my face with my good hand. "I could get used to it, too."

"Just kiss already," Misty said from somewhere to my left. I looked past Blaze's shoulder and saw Mabel was still lying on the floor, though face up this time, and all the overhead lights had been turned on. Stetson's voice rumbled through the doorway as he spoke into his cellphone. Mabel's quiet sobs made it difficult to understand him.

Feeling myself start to black out again, I looked back at Blaze, who was still gazing down at me. "Well, are you going to or not?" I demanded.

He laughed, the rich sound making me smile. "Don't ever change," he told me before obeying, and when I passed out that time, the last thing I knew was his lips moving over mine. I promised myself that when I woke up, I was grabbing him tight and never letting go. Almost getting killed does that to a person. It puts everything into perspective, and no way was I passing up a chance with Blaze.

My second blackout only lasted a few minutes, and when I came to, I was in the living room on the couch. Mabel stood by the door, hands zip-tied together behind her back, a solemn Stetson reading her rights to her. When he finished, he grabbed her shoulder and started to lead her out the door. The black sky pressed against the windows, but I had to know her reason for all the horrible things she'd done. Pushing away from Blaze as he held an ice pack to my arm while Misty talked to Jeff on her phone, I stood.

"Wait," I said, taking a few feeble steps. "Blaze, I need to talk to her."

Stetson hesitated, looking past me, Mabel's head bent, her shoulders slumped, and when Blaze gave him the go ahead, he led Mabel to the dining room table. The same table she and I had played games at only hours earlier.

"Jeff is on his way," Misty said, entering the room, her green eyes bloodshot. "I don't know how you're functioning with that busted arm, but I'm with you. We need to know now, before this goes to the press."

Gingerly, I eased into a chair across from Mabel, Misty next me, Blaze behind me, his hands on the back of my chair while Stetson stood behind Mabel, one hand on the butt of his gun as if he expected her to try something at any moment. From the way her head hung, chin almost touching her chest, I knew she was done fighting, and after summoning up every last bit of courage I had, I spoke.

"Mabel?" I whispered to the woman I had thought was one of my dearest friends. "Mabel, why?" My voice sounded broken, even to me, and before she lifted her head, tears ran down my cheeks.

"It was an accident," she said softly, all life gone from her brown eyes as they met my blue ones. Her hair was mussed and ratted around her face, her night shirt sporting a tear across one shoulder, and she had rug burn on her chin. "I didn't mean to kill Vicki. It just happened."

"What happened?" Blaze asked from behind me, and in his voice, I heard not the tone of a police officer but the tone of a friend.

Mabel looked down at the table, hands still zip-tied behind her back. "I was really sick of working for the insurance company, of always being told what to do instead of being in charge. I missed my old job of being a clown, so I asked Vicki how she would feel about me being a clown at her diner, just for kicks."

"I can't imagine that went over well," I said drily. Blaze gave my neck a warning squeeze, but since Mabel was more likely to talk to me than him, I ignored it.

Mabel shook her head. "She laughed at me. Pointed a finger in my face and mocked me. I'd come in really early, all dressed up, to show her, and she made fun of me, told me I was nothing more than a washed-up wanna be, and I'd never be anything more than a three-inch tall loser who painted her face. She said I should ask you, because having a clown around was a sure-fire way to run a business into the ground."

The urge to punch Vicki, dead or not, was strong, because that was just like her to say something like that. And apparently, Misty felt the same way about punching Vicki, because she muttered something under her breath.

"I got angry, really angry, and before I knew what I was doing, I'd grabbed up a rolling pin and hit her in the head with it," Mabel went on, and shaking her head, she stopped Blaze from speaking, having heard his inhale. "Yes, Blaze, this is my official confession. You can take it all down and use it against me. I can't take this anymore. I killed Vicki."

"You're the one who stole my cookbook, aren't you?" I said.

"You somehow got ahold of the code for the safe and stole it, then planted it to make it look like I'd killed her."

"Yeah," Mabel sighed, and behind her, Stetson shifted. The sudden movement startled me. "I didn't know what else to do, so I framed you. I watched you enter the code to your safe one time and your back-door lock was just loose enough that I could jerk on the handle and get it to open, which is how I got in both times. I hid the rolling pin at Cody's the morning of the Fourth, along with the drugs. It wasn't hard, since everyone was too busy setting up to notice. Someone had left the barn unlocked, and it was only a matter of placing a few plants and the rolling pin. Setting the fire that night was easy. No one saw me running away from the barn right before it started smoking because they were all packing up to leave. Since my efforts to frame Lacey hadn't worked, I knew Cody was probably my last chance."

"Why not just leave it at pretending you knew nothing about Vicki?" Misty asked her, leaning forward, the overhead light feeling harsh to my swollen eyes. "No one would have been the wiser, so why try to kill Aubrey? Why do everything you did, going to crazy extremes to buy drugs and cut through her steps? Why go that far?"

Mabel started crying, and the tears that I had thought I'd stopped up started pouring down my face again. "I hate my job," she sobbed. "All I ever wanted to be besides a clown is a baker."

"You could have been," I exclaimed. "I asked you to join me countless times."

"No!" Mabel yelled, eyes now lit with anger, lips quivering. "I would have been working for you. It's not the same. I could have had everything I ever wanted, until you came to town and ruined it."

"I don't get it," Blaze said. "That was years ago. Why act out now?"

"That building," Mabel went on, ignoring him, "that building you have, Aubrey. Who do you think was the unnamed person you outbid on it?"

I let out my own sob. "No. It wasn't you. It was Vicki. I know it was her."

"No. It was me." Mabel scowled. "You took every last hope I had of having a bakery, because no way could this town support three bakeries. But I forgave you." She heaved a sigh, looking for all the world like she might fall apart. "I forgave you, because I knew it wasn't your fault. Then, last week, when I killed Vicki, I realized how easy it is to get rid of people." She looked back at me. "I wasn't going to hurt you, I swear, and I wasn't going to frame you, but I remembered that about a year ago you told me you'd willed the business to me, and with Vicki gone, I'd have no competition. It's all I ever wanted."

I leaned back in my chair, shocked. Somewhere, somehow, Mabel's mind had snapped, and it was clear she wasn't the person she had once been. I tilted my head back to look up at Blaze, finding no words to speak, and he took over.

"You needed someone to take the blame for Aubrey's death," he said. "So, you broke into Lacey's shop and used her Eiffel Tower figurine to hit Aubrey in the head, knowing that I would investigate each and every shop until I found the murder weapon, but Lacey had a solid alibi. That's why the footprints outside her window were so faint. They were yours. When that didn't work, you started framing everyone, including Jesse, who, by the way, was my top suspect up until a few hours ago. That's why I thought Aubrey was safe out here."

He paused for a moment, seemingly to collect his thoughts. "Eventually, you pointed the finger at Cody, planting drugs on his property, which would make it look like he'd killed Vicki for breaking up with her because she found out about it. But I just can't understand why you acted like you did, trying so hard to find out who the killer was, going so far as to break into people's homes, when you knew good and well you wouldn't find anything.

"Why go through all that work if you were just going to try to kill Aubrey again? And more than that, why frame Jesse? Why leave me that anonymous false tip that he'd lied about his whereabouts when Vicki died?" His voice lowered. "Why not just kill Aubrey and pretend the killer had been a psycho who'd just been passing through?"

"I wanted her dead," Mabel said. "I didn't at first, but, once I realized how much I had to gain ..." She trailed off, then started up again. "The reason I tried so hard to find the killer and act like my heart was breaking for Vicki was so nobody would suspect me. Why would you when I'm doing everything I can to investigate and keep people safe?" Her voice was flat, emotionless, but her eyes were filled with pain as she realized exactly what she had done.

"I'd already killed one person. It wouldn't be that hard to kill a second, even if it took a few tries. It wasn't difficult to sweep the ground after I put the ladder back in the shed behind Jesse's and hide the saw in my house. Everyone was so worn out from the Fourth that I could have set off fireworks, and they wouldn't have heard me." She looked at the tabletop, her face a blurred reflection in its shiny finish. "I had to frame someone, Blaze. If I hadn't, you would have figured it out. Might have taken you awhile, but sooner or later, I knew you'd somehow figure it out. I couldn't afford that."

"Well," Blaze said, Stetson nodding, "you almost had me fooled into thinking it was Jesse after all. It was his place we'd been staking out at night, not yours. There was so much evidence piled against what he'd told us. We were sure it was him ..." Blaze's voice trailed off.

Misty shook her head as I faced Mabel again. "But, Blaze, what made you finally suspect Mabel?"

"Yes," Jeff's voice echoed through the house as he came in. "Tell us."

He sat down in the chair next to me after nudging Misty out of it and opened his medical bag. "What made you think it could be her?"

"She was too emotional at the memorial service," I blurted out, and I could almost feel Blaze staring at the top of my head. "I thought it was weird but blamed it on the fact grief affects everyone differently, but looking back, I realize it's because she felt guilty, not sad."

"Right," Blaze said. "It made me do a double-take, but then so much evidence came in against Jesse, we were swamped trying to sort it all." He sighed. "I'll give you that, Mabel. You were thorough. Took us days to clear it up as false, and up until a few hours ago, we were ready to arrest him."

"It was when she was dressed up as a clown at Cody's on the Fourth and tried to swat that bug," Stetson said. "Didn't really register as important at the time, but when things started falling together tonight, we realized there was a pretty big finger pointing at her." He rubbed his chin. "There was a sneaker skid on both yours and Vicki's kitchen floors, and when Mabel swung at that bug, her foot slipped forward, and left a skid mark in the dirt. I followed it up to see if there was anything else that looked wrong, but I hit a roadblock when I went to her employer and her internet provider to start double checking the times she said she was working. I didn't get the go ahead until this morning, and it was when we were on our way back tonight that the FBI got back to me."

"She was wearing stilts." My voice rose slightly. "Mabel, you were wearing stilts when you hit me so that you could actually reach my head."

"Yes," she replied, scrubbing her cheek on her shoulder. "Lost my balance and left that skid mark, but I didn't know about it until later when Brey was scrubbing at it." She glared at Blaze. "I didn't know there was one on Vicki's floor, either."

Jeff started arranging my arm into a temporary splint after giving me some painkillers. "What about your car?" he asked quietly.

"I cut the brake lines and let it hit a tree across the road," Mabel told him. "Rolled in the dirt and tore my clothes up to make it look like I'd jumped out of it."

"Another thing I found out almost too late," Blaze said. "I had your car towed to a mechanic over by Praline and he got ahold me when I was on site for the bomb threat you called into that concert three counties over. Told me no way could someone have cut the brake lines on your car unless they took off the front bumper or had really small hands." He paused when I drew in a sharp breath at Jeff's administrations. "That's when I knew for sure it was you."

"You were almost too late," Misty told him. "Thank God Aubrey woke up."

"How much time will she do?" I asked Blaze since it was clear Mabel had shut down for good, staring at the table again, tears streaming down her pink face.

"Life, most likely," he replied. "Mabel, you've got multiple charges of attempted murder on your hands, along with murder, assault and battery, lying to an officer of the law, resisting arrest, possession of an illegal substance, the framing of an innocent person with said illegal substances, and arson. Once I get everything written up and the Feds are done with you, there'll be a few more, so, chances are, you're going to get life."

A knock came to the door, and Stetson moved toward it. "That's probably them right now, coming over from where she called that bomb threat into so that Stetson and I would be out of the way assisting the other police force," he said. When he came back, he was followed by two severe looking men who wore FBI badges around their necks and neatly pressed suits. After a brief interview they led Mabel away. While Blaze helped me outside to his truck to take me to the clinic so Jeff could actually treat me, the agents loaded Mabel into the back of a black SUV. She looked back as they helped her climb in, and her soft words carried across the driveway to me. "I'm sorry, Aubrey. I'm so sorry."

"So am I." *Sorry I ever met you.* I wasn't really, but I knew there would be a lot of emotions to deal with, and anger led the pack. I would never regret the years I'd spent with Mabel, the laughter we'd shared, and I wouldn't even be remorseful about the past day, because I knew Mabel was sick, and no amount of my anger could cure her. That was something only God could do.

Feeling faint, I leaned against Blaze as the SUV roared to life and disappeared down the road. "I truly hope she gets the help she needs," I murmured as the edges of my vision started to turn gray.

Blaze started to speak but ended up catching me instead as I fell, and for the third time that night, my world went black.

16

Two weeks after Mabel's arrest, I sat on Blaze's back porch, enjoying a glass of iced tea while he played football with Stetson and Jesse, the new hire covering the station under Terri's stern eye.

"Jesse," I called to the shopkeeper. "You got a minute?"

Tossing the ball to Stetson, he stepped up onto the porch and sat next to me, breathing hard. "What's up?"

I met his kind gaze. "I need to tell you something. I'm the one who broke into your apartment."

Staring out across the yard, he nodded. "I know."

Surprised, I stared at him. "What do you mean you know?"

Pouring a glass of tea from the pitcher on the table next to me, he smiled. "I know you, Aubrey. As soon as I got home and walked into my apartment, I could tell someone had been in there. It didn't take much to figure out who and why."

"I'm so sorry," I told him, tears pricking my eyes. "That's not who I am. I have no excuse."

Setting the glass of tea down after taking a sip, he gave me a slight smile. "I know that, too. And it's all forgiven." Standing, he headed back out into the yard, wrestling the football from Stetson. I smiled as they joked around.

Hearing my cellphone chime, I picked it up from the table. It was Mitch. He and Kasey had returned to L.A. but kept in daily contact with me. He'd sent me a link to a story a prestigious newspaper had done on Flamingo Springs, Mabel's crime catching the interest of several news outlets across the country.

After I texted him back, I put my phone down and closed my eyes, enjoying the slight breeze the overhead fan provided.

"You throw like a girl!" Jesse yelled at Stetson as they wrestled over the ball, and Blaze laughed as he joined me on the porch.

"Like watching two kids," he said, wiping his sweaty forehead with the hem of his shirt before grabbing my glass of sweet tea and downing it.

I didn't even bother to protest since this wasn't the first time he'd pulled that stunt. He sat next to me, and we watched as Stetson and Jesse threw the ball back and forth, jeering at each other.

"You planning on watching Cody ride tonight?" I refilled my glass. "He's been in the upper eighties the last three nights."

"Probably," Blaze replied. I knew we were both glad the bull rider had been innocent.

It was silent on the porch for a while, and I leaned my head on his shoulder. "Life is good."

He rested his hand on my thigh. "I would say it can't get any better, but ..." he leaned forward and dug in his pocket. "It can."

Turning toward me, he handed me a little box. Balancing it on my knee so I could open it with my good hand, I laughed as I pulled out a bracelet, the little charms dangling from it telling the story of the last month. There was a charm that looked like a speeding ticket, a rolling pin charm, a horseshoe, and a few more, but the one that caught my attention was the one with diamonds in it. It was a silver cupcake, and when Blaze had clasped it around my wrist, he looked into my eyes.

"Aubrey," he said, "I love you, and I believe in taking life slow, enjoying the little things, and I have every intention of kissing you under the stars every night starting sometime in the near future." He touched my cheek. "Maybe I'm old-fashioned for doing this, but would you be my girlfriend?"

My squeal had Stetson ducking for cover out in the yard as I threw my good arm around Blaze's neck and laid a kiss on him that could be heard a county over. "Would I? Cowboy, after everything we've been through, I can't think of anyone else I'd rather be with."

"Seal it with a kiss?" he teased, and when I obliged, catcalls filled the yard. I smiled against his lips, thinking I'd have to rename the title of the email I'd started to my mom earlier that morning. "Pancakes, Bacon, and a Side of Murder?" More like "Pancakes, Bacon, and a Side of Happily-Ever-After."

"Yes, please," I murmured against Blaze's lips.

Pulling me close as we looked back out across the yard, Blaze let out a contented sigh and I echoed him. We were home.

THE END

ABOUT THE AUTHOR

Keri Lynn discovered her love for writing before she'd even completed kindergarten, and that passion has only grown over the years. The youngest of four children, Keri loves poetry and Escape Rooms. She plans to one day swim with sharks. When the Wisconsin-born writer isn't busy creating new worlds, she can be found experimenting in the kitchen, writing music, and spending time with her family. Keri resides in Nashville, TN.

COMING SOON FROM KERI LYNN

Coming November 2022:

Not a Good Day for Namaste

A Texas-Sized Murder Mystery Book Two

Witnessing the hit and run of fellow Flamingo Springs resident Ryan wasn't how yoga instructor Misty Van Oepen planned on starting the Thanksgiving holidays. When Ryan's mysterious brother shows up along with a spree of crime, she decides it's up to her and fellow business owners Lacey and Jeni to find out what's going on.

After an attempt on Misty's life lands her in protective custody at deputy Stetson Owens' ranch, she finds herself in danger of losing her heart to the former bull rider. With time running out, will Misty succeed in discovering who's behind the attacks? Or will she fail and become the next victim?

NEW FROM SCRIVENINGS PRESS

Cake That!

by Heather Greer

Ten bakers. Nine days. Only one winner.

Competing on the *Cake That* baking show is a dream come true for
Livvy Miller, but debt on her cupcake truck and an expensive repair
make her question if it's one she should chase. Her best friend,
Tabitha, encourages Livvy to trust God to care for The Sugar Cube,
win or lose.

Family is everything to Evan Jones. His parents always gave up their
dreams so their children could achieve theirs. Winning *Cake
That* would let him give back some of what they've sacrificed by
allowing him to give them the trip they've always talked about but
could never afford.

As the contestants live and bake together, more than the competition heats up. Livvy and Evan have a spark from the start, but they're in it to win. Neither needs the distraction of romance. Unwanted attention from Will, another competitor, complicates matters. Stir in strange occurrences to the daily baking assignments, and everyone wonders if a saboteur is in the mix.

With the distractions inside and outside the *Cake That* kitchen, will Livvy or Evan rise above the rest and claim the prize? Or does God have more in store for them than they first imagined?

Cruise to Death

Sara L. Jameson

Winner of the 2020 Scrivenings Press

Get Pubbed Contest!

When opera singer Riley Williams agrees to sub as a musical-theater performer on a luxury Rhine/Moselle River boat cruise, she gets more than she bargained for. Not only does she have to come up with 250 Broadway songs, she must dance with the male passengers. Dance—

the subject she nearly failed in her conservatory courses, and the cause of her recent flop in an opera house. To make matters worse, she overhears two terrorists at a café in Antwerp, Belgium, discussing the transfer of deadly Agent X to the highest bioterrorist bidders.

Interpol Agent Jacob Coulter, an anti-terrorism desk analyst in Brussels, Belgium, insists on serving as an undercover agent after his best friend Noel is murdered by terrorists from the cell he infiltrated in Brussels. Shortly before Noel dies, he manages to tell Jacob snippets of the terrorists' plans. Plans that seem to involve the same river boat cruise Riley is on.

When Interpol learns of Riley's encounter with terrorists at the café, Jacob's supervisor insists he work with her to identify the terrorists and retrieve Agent X. But their relationship is fraught with distrust because of Riley's suspicious past and a romantic attraction neither of them wants.

MORE MYSTERIES FROM SCRIVENINGS PRESS

Blue Plate Special

by Award-winning Author Susan Page Davis

Book One of the True Blue Mysteries Series

Campbell McBride drives to her father's house in Murray, Kentucky, dreading telling him she's lost her job as an English professor. Her father, private investigator Bill McBride, isn't there or at his office in town. His brash young employee, Nick Emerson, says Bill hasn't come in this morning, but he did call the night before with news that he had a new case.

When her dad doesn't show up by late afternoon, Campbell and Nick decide to follow up on a phone number he'd jotted on a memo sheet. They learn who last spoke to her father, but they also find a dead body. The next day, Campbell files a missing persons report. When Bill's car is found, locked and empty in a secluded spot, she and Nick must get past their differences and work together to find him.

Ring of Death

Cozy Mystery

Dorey Cameron just wants to do her job. But that's nearly impossible when her dental patients don't show up for appointments. The bizarre accidents causing them not to appear can't be a coincidence. Someone is sabotaging her. But why?

Things take a terrible turn when vandalism, mugging and murder have the police pointing the finger at Dorey. Something in her possession must be worth killing for. If Dorey can't figure out the mystery in time, will she be the next victim?

September Shadows

Book One - Justice, Montana Series

A mystery

After the sudden death of their parents, Jess Thomas and her sisters, Sly and Maggie, start creating a new life for themselves. But when Sly is accused of a crime she didn't commit, the young sisters are threatened with separation through foster care. Jess is determined to prove Sly's innocence, even at the cost of her own life.

Cole McBride has been Jess's best friend since they were children. Now his feelings are deepening, just as Jess takes risks to protect her family. Can Cole convince Jess to trust him–and God–to help her?

Stay up-to-date on your favorite books and authors with our free e-newsletters.

ScriveningsPress.com

Made in the USA
Monee, IL
16 December 2023

49517445R00125